VAMPIRE WATCHMEN

SAMANTHA CARTER SERIES

By Tim O'Rourke:

Vampire Seeker
Vampire Watchmen

Vampire Flappers (novella)

Tim O'Rourke

VAMPIRE WATCHMEN

piatkus

For Lynda – who like Sammy Carter has taken me on many adventures!

PIATKUS

First published in Great Britain in 2014 by Piatkus

A CIP catalogue record for this book is available from the British Library.

ISBN 978-0-349-40214-7

Typeset in Sabon by Palimpsest Book Production Ltd, Falkirk, Stirlingshire
Printed and bound in Great Britain by Clays Ltd, St Ives plc

Papers used by Piatkus are from well-managed forests and other responsible sources.

Piatkus
An imprint of
Little, Brown Book Group
100 Victoria Embankment
London EC4Y 0DY

An Hachette UK Company
www.hachette.co.uk
www.piatkus.co.uk

ACKNOWLEDGEMENTS

Special thanks to my three brilliant sons, Joseph, Thomas and Zachary for simply being themselves. Just be you – that's what matters.

Thanks to the amazing team at Piatkus, Anna Boatman, Grace Menary-Winefield, Alice Wood and the many others for their help and encouragement and who believed in Samantha Carter and the gang from the beginning.

And of course my continued thanks to all of the loyal fans of my work who I chat with on Facebook and who make the lonely life of an author so much fun! Thank you!

Hugs

Tim x

FOREWORD

Prior to writing *Vampire Watchmen*, I was asked by my editor to write a short piece of bonus material. At that point all I knew about *Vampire Watchmen* was that Samantha Carter would be travelling back to the great plague of London in 1665–66. So in early January 2014, I sat down and began to write. Two days later, I had written approximately 10,000 words – a bit more than the 500 words I had originally been asked for! Why so much more? Because I love writing about Samantha Carter. I mean, she is an absolute dream and every time I sit with my laptop it isn't long before she is whisking me back in time on another adventure. Writing about Sammy is really that easy for me. In each of her adventures I become no more than a mere observer, someone close to a reporter as I close my eyes and watch Sammy and the gang kick arse hundreds of years in the past.

I have written over 30 novels in just three years. Like

any other author I have my favourite characters, but if I'm to be totally honest, none of them give me the sheer adrenaline rush that I feel when I'm writing about Sammy. She is utterly fearless, determined and smart – what more could I ask for in a character?

So that's why those 500 hundred words of bonus material became *Vampire Flappers*: I got swept along in the adventure. There she was, heading back to Aldgate Tube station in search of her friends just like I had gone in search of her. And before I knew what was happening I was traveling back to 1920s France – opening my eyes and finding myself in a smoke-filled bar in Paris.

In *Vampire Watchmen*, Sammy can't remember what happened in Paris, and has to keep guessing. So for those of you who haven't read *Vampire Flappers* yet, you now have a choice: You can skip to the back of the book and find out straight away or you can stay right here and guess along with Sammy!

Whatever you decide to do, I hope you find Samantha's next adventure as exciting as it was for me writing it down between the pages of this book.

Go get 'em Sammy!

Tim O'Rourke

PART ONE

Aldgate

1

They were monsters who preferred the night. For hundreds of years they had waited, becoming a part of the darkness that surrounded them. They lived below ground while the humans forged through history, creating lives, villages, towns then cities above. All the while the monsters bided their time, waiting for the moment they would go above ground. They roamed the darkness, their wide mouths full of teeth, each one a jagged point. White claws, razor-sharp. Eyes as black as the depths they hid in. They waited. They were patient.

But as time passed, some had been less so and they had crept from below ground and ventured into the world above. Here they had kept to the shadows, never venturing too far from their murky depths. They watched the humans from afar, still too timid to approach. The monsters fed on flesh, but it was always cold. They had yet to discover the true delights of warm flesh – of the hot sticky blood that surged through the veins of the living. So they fed on the dead and took what substance they could from them. They stole from graves, snatching bodies so as not to draw attention to themselves. And when there wasn't enough flesh, or the risk of discovery by the humans was too great, they ate each other. Their Pale Liege told them their time was not yet. But it would come. One night they would at last know the delights of warm human flesh.

But deep within his withered soul the Pale Liege had a memory of a distant enemy, one who lived only to destroy him and his kind. His enemy lived above ground and wasn't human. He walked in the light and the dark. But that darkness had to be absolute or he too would perish. The Pale Liege knew his enemy changed his skin in the light of the moon. If the humans discovered this, they would hunt him down. Yet the Skinturner cared for these humans – he wanted to protect them. That was the Skinturner's weakness and that was what would kill him.

So it was better to wait in the darkness until there was enough flesh to feed his subjects.

2

"Hey! You!" I called up the stairs leading off the Underground platform and on to the concourse area. The man who had told me to mind the gap was now gone. I glanced at the curved wall of the station and read the name fixed there. *Aldgate*. How had I got here again?

I fought to remember the last few hours of my life. I would be lucky – I could barely recall the last year. It had passed in a haze and when I tried to look back it was like staring through a sheet of frosted glass. The images of what had taken place in 1888 were there, but only just visible. I had to struggle to picture the preacher, Harry, Louise and Zoe. With eyes closed, I concentrated on what I had done this morning.

I had been woken once again by the cries of joy coming from Sally's room just down the hall from mine. I had rolled over, covering my head with my pillow, but the sound of her being shagged by the guy she had brought home last night jabbed at my eardrums like needlepoints. Why did she always get to have so much fun? I thought, ripping back my bedding. I guessed I'd had my fun back in 1888 with a cowboy named Harry. Just my luck I could barely remember it!

Wanting to be gone before Sally slunk into the kitchen, her cheeks flushed hot and her eyes half shut with a look of dreamy satisfaction in them, I headed for the shower. Once I was dressed I left the flat. I wandered the streets of London, pretending to be interested in the same old sights I had seen a thousand times before. I smoked one cigarette after another, flicking the smouldering butts into the gutters that were swollen with rain. As I had walked, collar of my coat turned up, my blond hair soaked black, I had tried yet again to bring to mind the events that had taken place in Colorado. Had I really become a member of a group – *pack* – of skin-turning werewolves who hunted down vampires? Had I really caught a vampire myself? It seemed all too incredible; no wonder my brain had tried to block it out. If it hadn't then perhaps I would have gone mad. Perhaps I'd already lost my mind? I'd spent the last year of my life living like a zombie, sitting in lectures at uni and gazing out of the window, wondering if I would ever travel back in time again and meet up with the friends I had made there. But would I even recognise them again?

Now I realised that as my mind had turned to vampires and the friends I had made in 1888, I had found myself once again standing outside Aldgate Tube Station. It seemed to pull me to it every time I left my flat, like it reached out with a set of invisible arms and dragged me. But there had been something special about today. The station had pulled me towards it for a reason. Exactly one year had passed since I had stepped on to a train and gone back in time. One year since a faceless stranger had wrapped his arms about me, enclosing me just like the station itself. That stranger had sent me to 1888. But why, and who was he? And was he the same man I had just been chasing? I opened my eyes and looked at the platform edge. Then it came to me. I had followed him into the station. He had caught my eye outside. I closed my eyes again, pressing my fingertips against my temples. Had he thrown something at me? I could see coins clicking against the pavement at my feet. The French francs I now held in my hand, perhaps? Had I been to Paris recently? Could I have forgotten that too? But the French used the euro now. Had they come from another time, just like the man who had thrown them? So many questions racing along the corridors of my mind but I was unable to find the answer to one of them.

I opened my eyes again, looking at the platform edge. I could remember myself teetering, arms pinwheeling as if I was going to fall on to the tracks beneath the wheels of an approaching train. He had pushed me. I had felt the flat of his hand between my shoulder blades. But he had changed his mind at the very last moment, pulling me back instead of pushing me under.

I placed the francs back into my coat pocket and raced up the stairs, taking two at a time. The sound of the leather soles of my boots echoed off the curved walls of the Underground Station. The coins jingled in my pocket. I glanced down at the desolate platform as the empty train slowly rattled into the tunnel. My brain felt like a fucking knot. The platform had been full of passengers. I had fought my way through them as I had gone after that man. There had been so many squeezed on to the platform I'd nearly been knocked into the path of the approaching train. But I was sure now he had saved me, gripped me by the back of the neck, yanking me away as I teetered on the edge. All of that had happened in a blink of an eye, so where had all the hundreds of passengers gone? How had they vacated the station so quickly? They hadn't boarded the train, as that would have left the station empty. With a sinking feeling in my heart, I knew it wasn't the other passengers who had gone – it was me who had vanished. Fearing I had lost time once again, I rushed on to the concourse. Just like the platforms beneath me the concourse was deserted. The gates on the barrier line were open. There was no ticket collector tonight. With my heart thumping in my chest, I walked slowly forward.

"Hello?"

There was no answer, just the sound of the wind howling

through the wide-open entrance at the front of the station. What looked like flakes of dust swirled inside, covering the floor with white, like snow. Raising one hand up before my eyes, I peered out into the night as I passed slowly through the open barrier line. I couldn't see any traffic – taxis or night buses – pass by outside. With my arm still raised before me, I glanced at my watch. It was 7:10 p.m. Commuter time. The only thing was, there were no commuters. There were no buses or taxis to take them home – nothing. Just the sound of the baying wind and what looked like dust swirling through the air at the front of the station. With my heart still pounding and my stomach clenched tight, I made my way to the entrance. Just as I reached it, a sudden gust of wind blew hard into the station, spraying my face and hands with the white dust. I turned away, covering my eyes, nose and mouth with my hands. As I stood hunched against the blast, I heard a sound. At first I thought it was the howl and roar of the wind that made my skin prickle with gooseflesh, but it wasn't. The sound was too shrill – too agonising. The noise I could hear was the sound of hundreds of people crying out in pain. My fear was that if I dared to check back over my shoulder, I would find that I had somehow fallen into the depths of hell, where those who had never seen the light were now being tormented in utter darkness.

The moans and groans of despair circled me, gripping my heart, as if squeezing the life from it. In my mind's eye, I could see an ocean of people writhing against each other, their limbs entangled like a giant knot of human flesh. Each of them was desperate to be free of their own personal torment. I took my hands from my face and opened my eyes. At once I wished that I could close them again, but couldn't. I staggered backwards, stifling a scream by forcing my fist into my mouth. The hideous images my mind had conjured up now seemed like the illustrations from a fairy-tale compared to what confronted me.

I was no longer at the entrance of Aldgate Tube Station. It had vanished. I was on Aldgate High Street. How could I be so sure? St Botolph Church was still standing, although it looked kinda different to the church I passed daily on my way to uni, older, and although it still had a tall tower, it was now built from wood, rather than the white and grey stone I remembered. There was a graveyard which was now so vast the gravestones protruded into the road at the front and sides of the church where buses and taxis should pass by. But there were no real roads, not like the ones I had walked across daily in London. These were covered with dirt and stone. What looked like rotting food and excrement flowed in the gutters. I covered my nose at the vile stench, although it wasn't the smell of the filth and dirt that made me want to gag. It was the sea of rotting corpses covering the road that stank so much. And just like in my mind the decaying corpses were entangled together in a mass of spoiling flesh. The faces of the dead were bloated: purple, black and blue. Lips puffed until they had cracked, revealing black gums beneath. Eyes rolled back in hollow sockets. There were men, women and children. Whatever had killed them had not discriminated between the sexes, the young or the old.

The white dust continued to swirl all about me, and I was grateful when it gusted so thick on the wind that it blocked the hideous view of the dead stretching away in the direction of the church. There was another sound I could hear, like metal being scraped across earth. It was digging. I made my way amongst and over the mountainous trail of rotting corpses, in the direction of the church and the sound of shovelling. It was night, but the sky glowed with an eerie orange tinge. Then, through the dust and the smoke, I could see fires burning ahead of me. Flames licked from a giant mound in the graveyard at the front of the church. I inched my way forward, a sweet smell like that of slow-cooking pork going some way to block out the stench of rotting flesh. Suddenly I stopped and looked ahead, blinking and rubbing smoke from my eyes. This was so fucked up. I could see what looked like four giant Wombles digging in the graveyard. Their faces were long and pointed, brown in colour and leathery-looking. These creatures wore long dark robes that billowed about them like giant wings. Two of the monsters dug at the ground with shovels, another drove long wooden stakes into the chests of the corpses and the last carried the dead and placed them into the fire that raged. I peered through my cold fingers again, my legs growing weak as

I realised what it was these strange-looking creatures were doing. They weren't burying the dead, they were digging them up, driving pointed wooden stakes into their black withered hearts, then incinerating them. I looked up into the night sky, my stomach knotting with revulsion, realising it wasn't white flakes of dust that swirled all around me, but the smouldering ash from the corpses the creatures were throwing into the fire.

I wanted to be free of this nightmare. I wanted to wake up back in Aldgate Tube Station. I wanted to be in my flat, listening to Sally scream with orgasmic delight. Anything had to be better than the sound of those shovels scraping across earth, the rip of dead flesh as those stakes were skewered into the hearts of the dead and the crackling of burning corpses. I turned to flee towards the station that was no longer there. My head was telling me that it would be waiting for me, although my heart was telling me that it hadn't been built yet, that the London Underground wouldn't be constructed for another two hundred years and when they did dig the tunnels out in 1876 the ground would be almost impenetrable because of all the corpses buried in deep pits. But how did I know this? I had never been one for history at school. I had spent most of my time staring out of the classroom window fantasising about the existence of vampires. And if I wasn't doing that I was clock-watching, counting down the minutes until I could slip away to the furthest reaches of the school yard and smoke a cigarette. What I wouldn't do for a smoke right now. I drove my hand into my coat pocket, but there were no pockets. I wasn't wearing a coat. I was wearing a long black flowing gown with a hood, just like those creatures. There was a noise, like the fluttering of wings. Startled, I looked up. One of those creatures with the Womble-like faces was now standing before me.

3

My hand instinctively slipped beneath my robes, where my fingers found a series of long sharpened wooden stakes that hung from a leather belt around my waist. Before my heart had even a chance to beat, one of those stakes was in my fist and aiming straight into the pointed face of the creature that now loomed before me. The creature was just as quick to respond, and had gripped my wrist tight with one gloved hand. It was then as I stared into its strange face I realised it wasn't made of flesh at all, but leather. It had large black eyes, the size of small saucers. What I saw before me was a mask of some kind, which had been stitched together.

"Who are you?" I breathed, trying to wrestle my wrist free.

Whoever was hidden behind the mask loosened his grip

on me. Then with his free hand the mask was pulled from over the face. "Welcome back, Samantha Carter." He smiled at me.

His face was familiar. I had seen in it my dreams – in my nightmares. Staring into his ice-blue eyes, I remembered. I had first laid eyes on this man in 1888 as he stood on an outcrop of rock, two gleaming pistols pointing at the bandit who had wanted to hurt me. I had killed the bandit's men. I had blown their faces off with my own pistols. The pistols I reached for instinctively, just like I had now reached for the stakes fastened about my waist beneath the robes. But how had I known they would be there? How had I known how to use guns back in 1888? Had I been to both periods in time before?

"Preacher?" I said, astonished.

He took me by the arm and steadied me.

I looked into his blue twinkling eyes. He still had the bushy white moustache that drooped over his top lip like a handlebar. How many nights had I lain in the darkness of my bedroom fighting to keep sight of the preacher in my mind. Fearing that if I forgot his face, I would forget everything that had happened to me in 1888 – fearing I would forget Harry. And if I had, what would I be left with, a constant itch at the back of my mind? I had been right to return to Aldgate Tube Station on the anniversary of the night I had first gone back to 1888. I had time-travelled again. The man who'd saved me from falling in front of the Tube train had brought me here. But this wasn't the Old West and it definitely wasn't 1888.

"Are you the preacher?" I breathed. "Is it really you?"

"You sound as if you have forgotten all about me." He smiled again beneath his overgrown moustache.

"I think I was about to." I looked up into his face. And as I did, I saw memories being played out in his eyes. I could see him gunning down vampires with gaping wounds for mouths. I could see the shots from his pistols flashing. As I stood hypnotised, I could feel the contradiction and the conflict in his heart. There was the human side to this man, the priest who could care and give hope, but there was another side – the monster. And once again, his eyes were yellow instead of blue. In a sudden flash of memory I saw the preacher as he had first revealed himself to me on the train – the night he had told me he was a werewolf. His pupils were now blood-red; thick white eyebrows curled up in points at his temples. His white moustache now spread over his face like an unkempt beard. His ears were longer – pointed like wolves'. He smiled at me, and his lips cracked open, showing raw flesh underneath and a set of jagged teeth.

"What kind of creature are you?" I had asked him then.

A Turnskin, had been his answer to me.

"What's a Turnskin?" I could now remember myself asking him.

"A hound of God," he had explained.

I blinked and the monster had gone and the preacher was staring back at me.

"Sammy, are you all right?" he asked, still holding my arm.

"Where am I?!" I asked over the sound of the roaring fire and shovelling behind me. "*When* am I?"

With sudden flecks of yellow sparking in the preacher's blue eyes before the firelight, he looked at me from beneath his hood and said, "It's November 1665 and London is in the grip of a great plague . . ."

"A plague?" Suddenly I felt woozy. "A plague of what?"

"Vampires," the preacher said.

And my world went black.

4

The Watchman stood at the door. The streets were quiet. The whole of London was quiet. The only sound was the hourly chime of the bells from the nearby church as the dead were brought out and buried. Those who had been wealthy enough to hire carts had fled London months ago with their belongings. Others who had been granted a certificate of health at the Old Bailey had left London for nearby villages weeks ago. But as the plague worsened those living in the surrounding villages and towns had refused to take any more evacuees. That was good for the Watchman. He wanted people to stay. While there were sick, he was employed. But it wasn't just the king's money the Watchman wanted. It was the flesh. Since the outbreak of the plague, the Watchman had seen many a strange thing as he stood night after night at the doors of the houses that had been marked with a red cross. He kept his back to that symbol always; he did not want to look at it. Standing outside so many houses across London, making sure those who were sick inside didn't leave and spread the plague, he had delighted at the death he had seen. He marvelled at the sight of those who rolled about in the filth-ridden streets as if being attacked by invisible adversaries. The Watchman had known very well what the sick were fighting off. Those who had first fallen ill had been bitten by infected rats that had come ashore on boats from Holland and Italy as they carried their goods up the Thames. But those infected vermin had died out months ago. It was another type of creature altogether spreading the plague now. And as the Watchman stood guard over those confined inside, he watched the dying convulse as in the last moments of their lives they remembered the creature that had bitten them, with his big grinning mouth and black gums crammed full with needle-like teeth, as he lunged at them, tearing the flesh from his victims' necks.

But other watchmen had come to London. Where they had come from, the Watchman didn't know. They were a different breed. These new watchmen had advised the king to tell his subjects to chew garlic. To wear it tied in posies about their necks. These new watchmen were dangerous. They were careful only to appear during the day, when he was sleeping – resting from the harsh glare of the sun. It had been a hot summer; the days and nights had been airless. The Watchman had needed to rest during the day, only seeking out his prey and spreading the sickness at night.

With only the sound of the distant tolling of the church bells to tell plague-ridden London it was midnight, the Watchman turned to face the door of the house he guarded. He kept his hood low, so as not to see the red cross marked on the door. Taking a key from his pocket, he unlocked the rusty padlock that fastened it. The young woman inside wasn't infected – not yet. Her mother had died, so had her baby brother, and her father was lying in one of the many pest houses that had been opened, places where the sick could suffer until they died.

The Watchman eased open the front door and stepped into the shabby house. Wooden beams crisscrossed the ceiling just above his head. The young girl was asleep. He had seen her shadow at the bedroom window snuff out the candlelight some time ago now. She was only to be held captive in the house for two more weeks before the doctor would come to give her a certificate of health so she could flee London if lucky enough to find a neighbouring village or town that would take her in. But she would never get to leave London, the Watchman thought as he slowly climbed the stairs to her room.

Her mistake had been to smile at him. She was so flirtatious. On the nights he had brought her food, she had lowered the basket from her bedroom window so he could place in it the bread and cake he had bought with the coins she had thrown from the window at him. On those nights she had worn little more than her white vest and petticoat. Even in the bitterly cold nights she had worn the same. It had been the sight of her smooth milky-coloured flesh the Watchman had liked. He could smell the soap on it even over the stench of the dying in the houses on each side of the street.

One night she had asked the Watchman to throw back his hood so she could look upon his face. She wanted to see the person who guarded her each night and bought her food. The Watchman was hesitant at first, for his face wouldn't be what the young woman was expecting. She was hoping her guard – saviour – was a handsome young man. But no such face lurked beneath the hood. Still, he wanted to look upon that flesh with his own eyes. So stepping slightly back into the shadows, the Watchman pulled back his hood. In the light of the pale moon his face was young and smooth enough to fool the young woman into believing he looked like a beautiful young man. She seemed delighted, as the Watchman couldn't but notice her look of desire. He lowered the hood again.

Now the Watchman stood in the corner of her bedroom, a sliver of moonlight filtering in through the window. He watched the fall and rise of her breasts as they strained beneath the thin fabric of her nightdress. The Watchman liked the sound of her beating heart, the smell of the blood pumping through it. He made his way across the room, stopping beside the bed. The young woman stirred, as if sensing in the furthest reaches of her sleep that she was no longer alone. The Watchman watched her eyelids flutter like butterfly wings as she opened her eyes. She gasped to find him standing there, in the pool of moonlight.

"Shhh," he whispered, and placed one long white finger against her lips. He traced the tip of his finger around her mouth, over her chin and down the length of her smooth neck. The Watchman could feel the blood pulsing through her carotid artery and couldn't be sure if she was scared or aroused by his presence in her room. Perhaps both. He smiled beneath the hood. With his free hand, the Watchman slowly pulled back the bedclothes. The young woman made no attempt to stop him, instead holding out her arms as if to welcome him into her bed – into her. Placing his hands on her thighs, he drew her legs apart, then up, so that they were bent at the knees. With trembling fingers, the young woman slowly hitched up her nightdress, revealing her fleshy thighs. The Watchman couldn't help but notice how in the moonlight, they looked as if they had been carved from marble. Climbing on to the bed, the Watchman positioned himself between her open legs. He stared down into the V-shaped strip of darkness before thrusting her legs further apart, letting moonlight pour on to her glistening wetness. Sighing, the Watchman sank between the young woman's legs. He lapped at her as she squirmed before him on the bed. He felt her hands go to his hood, and slowly pull it back. She wanted to look upon that beautiful young face again and those smooth lips that were now giving her so much pleasure. Gently,

she raised the Watchman's head so she could look into his dark eyes. Then, as if seeing his face for the first time, her face crumpled with a look of horror.

"Why, you're not a man at all," she gasped. "You're a—"

Before she had a chance to say anything more, the Watchman sank his head back between the young woman's legs as she began to scream.

5

"Does she remember this time?" I heard someone ask. The voice was female, young.

"Not in Paris, she didn't," another voice cut in. This one male, gruff-sounding. "It was like she'd forgotten everything. She barely remembered what happened in '88."

"We need to get inside," a female voice said. This one different to the first. "It's not safe for us to be out here at night."

I tried to open my eyes, but it was like they had been sewn shut. However much I willed them to open they wouldn't. The blackness hovered at the edges of my mind, and in it I could see a young woman screaming as she was eaten on a bed in an upstairs room of some ancient-looking house. Her face was screwed tight with pain as she tried to claw and kick at a monster crouched between her legs. I didn't want to see her face – I couldn't bear to look upon it. But I knew the only way I would rid my mind of her slaughter was to open my eyes. With all the strength I could muster, I forced my eyes open. Long black eyelashes flickered in my line of sight as I struggled to focus on the faces above me. I saw the preacher first, then I rolled my eyes from left to right. The one furthest to the right was pretty, young, and frowning. Her hair was long, blond and tied into two pigtails that hung over each of her cloaked shoulders. Now I could remember parts of what I had forgotten. Faces and names.

Zoe? Zoe Edgar? I wanted to say, but just couldn't form the words.

So Zoe hadn't been a figment of my imagination either. Would I have created her again if all this was in my mind? Maybe my imagination wasn't as creative as I believed it to be. I turned my head slightly. Another face. This one slightly older, but just as beautiful as the first and framed with long thick dark hair.

Louise Pearson?

Wasn't she a werewolf now? She had been bitten by Zoe outside the mine carved in the side of the Sangre de Cristo Mountains back in Colorado.

Back?

How did that work out?

Hadn't the preacher said I was now in the year 1665? That meant what happened to Louise, to me, to all of us in 1888, was *forward*, not back. I had to be making this shit up. Maybe that man at Aldgate Station had pushed me under the train after all. Only my scattered brain could construct something like this as I lay beneath its wheels in London of 2014 waiting for the paramedics to fight their way through the throng of commuters gawping down at my frying body sparking against the electric train tracks. I was dying and my mind was creating some kind of weird fantasy for me to hold on to as my life seeped from me. Didn't people say you were meant to head towards the light? But there wasn't any frigging light for me. Not that I could see. I tilted my head back towards the left and saw another face surveying me, this one that of a rugged-looking man. Fuck me, he was hot. Now that was more like it. If I were really dying, I wouldn't mind heading towards that face. It was better than any welcoming light.

"Harry?" I mumbled.

"I thought you said she didn't remember anything?" Zoe said.

"She certainly remembers you." Louise half smiled as she looked at him.

Harry simply shrugged his broad shoulders. "Typical doll, thinking about cock the whole time."

"Thinking about yours is she?" Louise nudged the preacher with her elbow.

"She just might be." Harry scowled, his forehead creasing, giving him that oh-so-moody-look.

Zoe looked away and back down at me. Had I once thought that she liked Harry – perhaps as more than just a friend? My brain felt like it had been put through a shredder. I looked at Harry again and he at me. Our eyes locked for just a moment. A smile formed at the corner of his lips, then faded as he quickly looked away. But I knew he was glad I was back, however much he tried to shrug my reappearance off.

"Hey Sammy, you okay?" Zoe asked, a sweet smile on her lips.

I nodded my head slowly, throat feeling raw, lips cracked. I ran the tip of my tongue over them.

"Give her some room," the preacher said, looping his arm through mine and easing me to my feet.

I stood beside him, swaying uneasily on my feet. "What happened?"

"You fainted," the preacher said.

"No, I meant what really happened to me?" I said, rubbing my temple with my fingertips. Smoke still billowed from the fire and the air still smelt of burning flesh.

"What do you mean?" Louise asked. She held one of those leather pointed-looking masks in her hand.

I looked at her, long dark hair whispering about the hood of her black cloak in the cold breeze. "Well, if I'm not mistaken, the last time I saw you, Louise Pearson, you were changing into a freaking werewolf. You spoke with a different accent, not the English one you have now." Before she could say anything, I teetered on my unsteady legs and addressed Zoe. "And you were the one who bit her. You were a werewolf too, Zoe Edgar." Then looking at the four of them, I added, "You were all werewolves – Skinturners."

"What else do you remember?" the preacher gently asked, as if coaxing a confession from me.

I glanced at Harry and my cheeks flushed hot. I could remember what had happened between us on that train. That had been hot too. I might have forgotten a lot, but not that. I looked away and back at the preacher. "I remember blowing myself to smithereens inside some gold mine as I fought with Jack the Ripper. Crazy, I know."

"Is it?" the preacher said.

"Yeah, you're right, it's not crazy. It's fucked up, that's what it is!" I snapped at him. "People just don't travel back in time to hunt down vampires. I'm making all this shit up. I know I am. I'm really back in 2014 dying or having some kinda frigging breakdown. And that's another thing!"

The preacher continued to look at me. "What is?"

"If I am making this crap up inside my head, why is it I never conjure up a packet of goddamn smokes!? I create every other kind of possible fantasy, but not a pack of cigarettes!"

Without taking his crystal-blue eyes from me, the preacher reached into the folds of his long black robes and fished out a cigarette that he must have brought with him from another time. It was a little bent. After straightening it, he held it up before me. I snatched it and popped it into the corner of my mouth, where it dangled. The preacher brought a match up to it and I drew in a deep lungful of smoke. It jetted from my nostrils.

"Better?" The preacher lit a smoke for himself.

"I guess. But a simple smoke doesn't make any of this – any of you – any more believable." I looked at all the dead bodies lying in the street, the raging fire and the corpses that burned within its seething flames. "I just don't believe what I'm seeing."

The preacher took a step closer to me. "We live by faith and not by sight," he said.

Suspecting he was quoting the Bible at me, I looked at the mound of bodies I had seen him and the others dig up from their graves. "Jesus said that one day we will all rise from the dead, but somehow I don't think he was talking about this."

"He also said that in hell the fire is never quenched."

"So this is hell then?" I asked, continuing to look down at the mass of decomposing bodies.

"It soon will be unless we stop the vampire who is paving the way for the Pale Liege."

I shook my head as if recollecting something I had once been told but had forgotten. "You told me about him before. He is like the king of the vampires."

"Right," the preacher said. "And I also told you once that although the vampires promise immortality it is not eternal life that they have to offer." Then glancing at the bodies smouldering in the fire, he whispered, "It is a living hell."

Without saying another word, the preacher headed in the direction of the church. The others followed, leaving me alone amongst the rotting corpses.

6

I followed behind as the preacher and the others made their way across the dark graveyard and towards the church. Gravestones either lay broken or smashed. Those that still remained upright leant precariously to one side, looking as if they might just tumble over at any moment. Mounds of earth covered the graveyard like it had come under attack by a plague of giant moles rather than vampires. Clouds of black smoke wafted between the scrawny trees, white ash coating everything it touched like a blanket of snow. The sky was covered with a bank of cloud. The edges of it shone blue, where the moon hid tucked away. It was then I understood why the preacher and the others were so keen to get back inside the church. Being in their company again was making what had happened between us grow clearer. It was like someone had wiped away the dust that had been building up in thick layers over my memories. I got the feeling that their urgency to be hidden away at night would grow as a full moon threatened. How many days or weeks until the next full moon, I didn't know. As I followed them at some distance, I remembered that during a full moon, each of them had to be locked away so that they couldn't kill. Hadn't Harry told me that the job of securing and watching over them had once been the job of a young woman named Marley? Hadn't she died somehow? Hadn't it then been the job of Louise to guard them? But she too was a wolf now. I didn't have to stretch my imagination too far to understand that role would fall on me if I were still around at the next full moon. I pressed the flats of my hands against my temples. With my eyes closed, I murmured to myself.

"If this is all a part of my imagination, please when I open my eyes let me be on some sun-drenched beach with Harry and let him be wearing the smallest pair of trunks . . ."

"Are you okay?" a voice suddenly asked me.

I snapped open my eyes to discover Zoe had hung back from the rest and was walking along beside me amongst the graves. There was no beach and no Harry strutting around like a Greek god in a pair of trunks so tight they would bring tears to his grey eyes. If I ever did discover I had any real control over this fantasy, the next time I went back through history I was gonna make sure I ended up in Ancient Egypt where I was some queen and Harry was my dumb manservant who had to obey every one of my sordid whims or fear being . . .

"You're doing that thing again," Zoe said, placing a hand to her pretty mouth as if to stop herself from giggling.

"What thing?" I said, taking one last puff of my cigarette and flicking the smouldering end away.

"Talking to yourself," Zoe said. "You're always talking to yourself."

I hadn't even realised I'd been talking out loud. Blushing at the thought Zoe might have heard my thoughts about Harry, I gently took her by the arm. "What do you mean, *always*?"

"Always." Zoe shrugged.

"You make it sound like this isn't only the second time I've come back. How many occasions has it been, Zoe?" I looked her straight in the eyes.

"I'm not sure I should be talking about this . . ." she started.

"Why not?" I glanced up to see that the preacher, Harry and Louise had reached the doors of the church. "How many times?"

"I can't remember," she said, pulling free of me and heading over to where the others waited for us.

"And neither can I," I muttered. Although Zoe's answer to my question had been more than vague, it suggested that I had travelled back in time more often than I could myself remember. But why couldn't I? Why had I almost forgotten my journey back to 1888? And as I made my way towards the church, I knew that if I hadn't come back now to the preacher and the others, it would have only been a matter of a week or two, perhaps a month, before I had forgotten all about them again. If this was just an innocent fantasy created by myself, why not imagine somewhere nice instead of vampire-infested gold mines and plague-ridden graveyards?

The preacher ushered us inside and closed the pair of wooden doors behind us. He locked them with a heavy-looking brass key. He then slid three bolts closed. I suddenly felt entombed, a prisoner. I looked about the church. It was constructed from thick timber, which rose high above me in a series of beams. An aisle ran up the centre, rows of pews stretching away on each side. The church was lit by an array of candles fixed into several large ornate candle holders. Each of them held about twenty or more candles. Wax ran in clots down the sides of them, their flames flickering back and forth as the wind began to blow harder outside.

Brushing past me, the preacher made his way up the aisle towards a small stone altar. Was this where he gave his sermon each Sunday morning? Somehow I doubted it. He didn't appear to be that type of preacher. At the altar he bowed before a crucifix on the wall. Christ didn't look in peace as he hung from the cross, he looked in utter agony. I spied the preacher make the sign of the cross over his heart. He then made his way behind the altar. The others followed without the reverence the preacher had shown. I followed too, one eye on the crucifix. To look up at it reminded me of the rosary beads I had found in the chapel in the town of Black Water Gap back in 1888 – or was that *forward*? I'd had them on me as I'd entered Aldgate Underground in 2014. They had been the only tangible proof of my time-travel.

We live by faith and not by sight, I heard the preacher's voice as if he were inside my head.

I checked my pockets for the rosary beads. But the black shroud I was wearing had no pockets, just a belt that held an array of finely pointed stakes. The thought of not having the rosary beads caused a sudden spike of panic deep inside of me. Wouldn't the preacher have reminded me that I didn't really need the rosary beads – all I really needed was a little faith?

I pushed his doctrine from my head as I passed behind the altar and watched as the preacher pulled open a door set into the wall beneath the crucifix. The door was made from the same colour wood as the wall. If you hadn't known of its existence, the doorway would have been invisible to the casual observer. Stooping low, the preacher disappeared through the opening. Harry followed, as did Louise and Zoe. I stood before it, heart starting to speed up a little. What did I have to be scared of? Looking back just once into the dimly lit church, I stepped into the darkness on the other side of the door and closed it behind me.

7

A set of stone stairs spiralled away into a pit of darkness. Even the candles that flickered from the stone walls did nothing to light the gloom down there. The preacher plucked a candle from a holder and led us down a narrow passage, away from the stone steps. I followed the others, the hem of my long black cloak swishing over the cobbled ground beneath me. The sounds of our shoes echoed off the stone walls and it reminded me of the Underground tunnels in 2014. Was part of me still there? Was I really lying beneath that Tube train or had I simply vanished in front of all those other commuters before the train had struck me? Had I been saved by that faceless man? Was he my friend or enemy? I believed it had been he who had sent me back to 1888. But how many times had he done this and how many different places had I been sent to? After talking to Zoe as we had crossed the graveyard, I was beginning to suspect I'd been hanging out with the preacher and his gang of vampire seekers more than I cared – *dared* – to remember. Had terrible things happened to me? Had I done terrible things myself? From my studies in criminology I knew that some killers chose to forget their crimes and their victims chose to forget the crimes committed against them. It was like we all had a built-in safety valve which cut off those memories that would cause us trauma. But one thing was for sure: we all remembered the killers and soon forgot about the victims. So had my mind thrown a cut-off switch somewhere? Since returning from 1888 my sleep had sometimes been plagued with visions of me killing men – shooting them in the face – the backs of their heads breaking apart like a dropped egg. But as I sat alone in the middle of the night and struggled to remember those men, something deep inside said that they would've hurt me if I hadn't killed them. Yet how had I ever learnt to use guns, a dagger?

Dagger?

Had I used a dagger? When? Where?

I suddenly wanted to reach for my thigh as if I instinctively knew I would find a dagger concealed there. Just like I had known there was a belt of stakes hidden beneath my black flowing robes. My hand trembled and I reached for the cold stone wall to steady myself. I shut my eyes. A hideous image of a female with a dagger protruding from her eye flapped across my mind, then was gone.

"Sammy?" I heard a voice ask as if coming from the far end of the passageway the preacher led us through.

I opened my eyes to see Zoe, standing beside me, the nearby flicker of candlelight giving her face a warm glow. "I just feel a bit dizzy," I said, easing myself from off the wall.

"That can happen," she said.

I looked at her. "What can?"

"Feeling dizzy. Shifting can make you feel like that sometimes . . ." Zoe stopped as if realising she had said too much, then turned and headed back down the passageway.

"Shifting?" I called after her. "What the fuck is *shifting*?"

As I watched Zoe catch up with the others I got the feeling she wanted to tell me what was really happening, but something or someone was stopping her from doing so. Zoe was a sweet girl. How old was she? Sixteen? Seventeen? No older than that. As I started after her, I could vaguely recall Zoe telling me once, as we travelled on that train up into the mountains, that her entire family had been killed by vampires. It had been the preacher who had saved her. She owed him her life and perhaps her silence too. I knew I would have to get her alone.

We reached the end of the passageway and another door. The preacher swung it open and revealed a snug-looking room. Just like in the rest of the building the floor was made of stone, but here a roughly woven rug had been thrown over it. There were several chairs, a table and a pile of smouldering embers in the fireplace. The window was covered with a curtain. To block out any moonlight, perhaps? There were two other doors and a wooden staircase leading up into darkness. I guessed this house was where the preacher and the gang lived in 1665. Louise opened one of the doors and walked into another room. The front door to the house was locked securely with a series of sturdy-looking bolts.

"Take a seat, Sammy," the preacher said, gesturing towards a chair by the fire.

I dropped into it. He handed me a smoke. Louise came back into the room carrying a tray which she placed on the table. With her fingers she shredded the cooked partridge and shared the meat out on to some plates. She then added some vegetables and handed me one of the plates of food. It looked and smelt better than the pink pulp I had been given to eat back – *forward* – in 1888. However much I tried, I would never be able to forget that stuff.

"Drink?" Louise asked.

"Got coffee?" I was unsure if it was drunk in 1665.

"We have tea," Zoe cut in. "The queen brought it with her from Portugal. She has made it very fashionable here."

"Then I shall have that."

She fetched me a cup of tea. As I sat and picked at the food, I looked across the room at Harry who sat at the table.

With his hood back, I could see his sandy-coloured hair was cut collar-length short, but as scruffy as ever. The lower half of his face was shadowed with short whiskers. He sat silently and chewed his food, as the preacher sat in a chair opposite me and smoked. He threw the cigarette butt into the glowing embers and lit another almost at once. Louise came and rested on the arm of his chair, and he placed his hand over her thigh. Hadn't they been lovers? Hadn't they shagged as loud and as often as Sally and her cop boyfriends?

Zoe came and sat on the rug, crossing her legs at the ankles as she warmed herself before the fireplace. A heavy silence hung over the room, and I began to feel uncomfortable. I pulled a fleshy piece of meat from the bone and popped it into my mouth. I really wasn't very hungry. In fact the food was pretty tasteless. I washed the meat down with a mouthful of warm tea. With the silence becoming almost deafening, I looked up at the preacher. His hand had slid further up Louise's thigh and he was casually stroking the flesh beneath her dark robes with his strong-looking fingers.

"You said this was the year 1665, right?" I asked, placing my plate to one side.

"Right," the preacher said, taking the cigarette that dangled from beneath his white moustache and handing it to me.

I took it from him and smoked. "Now my history might not be up to much, but I do know enough to realise that

I've come back in time smack-bang in the middle of the great plague of London. Correct?"

"Correct." He continued to paw Louise's thigh.

"The people of this time buried those who died of the plague in death pits – mass graves," I said, wishing again that I had paid more attention in my history lessons at school.

The preacher nodded and lit yet another smoke. Zoe watched me from the floor, and Harry from the chair on the other side of the room. The wind rattled the window and doors in their frames.

"So what I can't figure out is why you were digging up those corpses, staking them, then tossing them into the fire," I asked. "Do you suspect they're all vampires?"

"Some of them," the preacher said. "But we can't be sure which ones are. Some of the more decomposed, the ones with their throats ripped out, I doubt will come back from the dead, but the ones with the black tokens have to be staked . . . we can't take the risk—"

"Black tokens?" I cut in.

"Puncture wounds. Bite marks." He placed his hand to his neck. "Those ones, we just can't risk leaving them lying about."

"But they weren't exactly lying about," I reminded him. "They were dead and buried until you dug them up again."

"Buried, yes," he said. "Dead? Not always. The bodies we find with black tokens on their flesh, we stake and burn. The others we just leave in the street."

"In the street!" I almost choked on a throat full of smoke.

"You'll understand soon enough," the preacher said.

"Why dig them up at all?" I asked.

Harry suddenly spoke up. "Because those death pits are becoming banquets for the vampires."

I looked at him.

"Vampires haven't always lived above ground," Harry said, pushing his chair back from the table and standing up. There was a jug on the table and he poured some of its contents into a mug. It smelt like overripe apples and I guessed it was cider he was drinking. He armed some away from his top lip, then came and sat on the floor by the fire beside Zoe.

"So where did they live?" I asked him.

"Below ground, like the vermin they really are."

"So the history books got it wrong then?" I asked. "The plague wasn't started by rats, but by vampires?"

"The history books are right about the rats bringing the plague to London on boats," Louise started to explain, the Preacher's hand now lying palm down against her thigh. "But they died out during the cold winter months. They left behind thousands of victims, who as you know were buried in mass graves in an attempt to stop the spread of the plague. But so many dead bodies buried in such a cluster caught the attention of the vampires. For hundreds of years they had lain dormant in their caves below ground – but the scent of warm decaying corpses in such great numbers reawakened their hunger and thirst for human blood."

"So by digging up the dead bodies, you are depriving the vampires of food – of human flesh?" I breathed, as if the last piece of a jigsaw puzzle had fallen into place.

"See, I knew Sammy didn't just think about cock all the time," Zoe said, scowling at Harry. "She's just as smart as any of us."

Harry said nothing and took another swig of cider from the clay mug he held in his huge fist. I couldn't help but notice the quick look he shot me over the rim of the mug as he brought it up to his lips.

I looked back at the preacher. "So is starving the vampires working?"

"It was." He sighed with something close to regret. "The number of plague deaths began to drop each week. We advised the king that those who hadn't fled London should wear garlic about their necks, wear it as posies, wear leather pointed masks full of the stuff . . ." He pointed down at his own mask which lay at his feet.

"Hang on a minute," I cut in, sitting forward in my seat. "Did you say the king?"

"King Charles the Second, to be precise," the preacher said, unfazed. "To him, I'm just a simple man of the cloth who has a knack of understanding how to prevent the spread of the plague."

"So he knows about the vampires?" I asked him.

"No, he would cut off our heads if we spoke of such

wild things. He doesn't have any idea what we truly are or what or who his enemy is. He believes I work miracles through prayer."

"So he believes everything you tell him? He takes your advice?"

"The king is a man of faith, a Catholic at heart, although he declares himself a Protestant to his subjects," the Preacher explained. "His wife is a Catholic and so is his brother James."

"His brother is hot," Zoe cut in with a giggle.

Everyone ignored Zoe's remark, and the preacher continued.

"The king and his court trust me; I am a holy man after all, am I not?" He smiled at me. His eyes said differently. "As Jesus said, he who knows my teachings and does them, is a wise man."

"But you said your efforts to get rid of this vampire plague are no longer working?"

"Yes, and the king grows suspicious of us," Zoe cut in again.

Everyone in the room shot a glance at her. She almost seemed to wilt beneath our stares.

"You are quite right, Zoe," the preacher said. "Just when it looked like we had the plague under control – beaten – it started to flourish again."

"How?" I asked.

"I suspect the Pale Liege has sent one of his own, perhaps several, to spread the plague once more," the preacher explained. “We are having bodies brought to us that already show the signs of being bitten before they are even buried in the death pits. The carts that are being brought to us each day are full of corpses which have been drained clean of blood or mutilated beyond all recognition. The plague victims are no longer dying of the plague but of hideous mutilations. They are being eaten.”

I sat back in my chair, feeling dazed again.

“Are you okay?” the preacher asked. “You look suddenly ill, Sammy.”

“She felt dizzy when we were in the passageway,” Zoe said kneeling up beside me and taking one of my hands in hers.

“*Shifting*, right?” I whispered, glancing up into her eyes.

Zoe’s pretty face flushed red, and she silently pleaded with me not to say a word. I kept what she had let slip to me our secret, for now anyway.

“I’m fine,” I said, taking another sip of the tea, which had now turned cold. “Just tired I guess.”

“Perhaps then we should sleep now,” Louise said, looking at the preacher. The sparkle in her eyes told me that she had no intention of sleeping if she and the preacher headed off to bed.

Not intending to spoil her fun, but just wanting to find out as much as I could about the here and now that I found myself in, I looked at the preacher and said, “I’m fine, really. Tell me more about the vampires.”

I saw the look of disappointment dim the bright glow

in Louise's eyes, understanding all too well the knot of frustration Louise would now be feeling.

The preacher started to talk again, picking up from where he had stopped. "So the king grows tired and I fear suspicious of us as the body count begins to rise once again."

"Why does this Pale Liege only send one, possibly two or three vampires above ground?" I asked him. "Why doesn't he send more?"

"Because he fears me," the preacher said. "He fears us – he fears Skinturners. We have beaten his kind before. The vampires' number is greater but so are their weaknesses. They are vulnerable during daylight, we are not. The Pale Liege won't risk coming for us. He won't want to reveal himself or his kind. He will want someone else to do his dirty work. Then when we are dead, he will strike."

"He wants the king to grow suspicious of you," I decided. "He wants the king to have you killed."

"Sammy has it all figured out," said Zoe.

"Thank you." I smiled at Zoe, then glared at Harry. He glared right back.

"So now you know everything, Sammy." Louise yawned, gripping the preacher's hand that rested against her thigh. She stood up, half pulling him out of his seat.

"Hang on," I sighed. "I don't know everything."

"No?" The preacher regarded me sternly. "What else is there to know?"

"Why am I here?" I demanded.

Before he had a chance to answer my question, there was a thunderous bang on the front door.

A voice boomed from the darkness outside. "Open up, preacher man!"

8

We were all up on our feet before the voice outside had stopped ringing in our ears. I looked down and could see one of those sharp wooden stakes in each of my fists, not even aware that I had reached for them.

The preacher edged towards the door, Harry right behind him. There was a tense atmosphere in the small house now. Zoe and Louise stood in the centre of the room, their long slender fingers turned to claws. I looked at Harry and the preacher. Their hands looked unnaturally big, fingers thick and long, each capped with an ivory-looking claw. I could feel my heart beating in my ears. I took a deep breath as I scanned the room, for ways of escape and anything else I could use as weapons other than the stakes I held. I had had similar if not the same feelings before, in 1888. My sense of survival had seemed inflamed back there, just like it did now. It was as if there was another secret part of me, a dangerous, reckless, violent side that revealed itself when I travelled back in time and found myself in the company of my new friends.

Another bang on the door, causing it to shake in its frame.

The preacher glanced back over his shoulder at us. "Ready?" he mouthed. And as he opened his mouth I could see that his gums were now swollen with rows of jagged teeth. His moustache was thicker too, white fur spreading out across his face, giving him a wild beard that only his bright blue eyes shone through. Harry gave a nod, to signal that he was ready for anything. I could see that Harry's hair was now thicker, darker and scruffier than before. He had a wild set of bushy sideburns that covered his firm jawline.

"Preacher!" the voice roared from the other side of the door again.

All four of my friends snarled, each brandishing a mouthful of pointed teeth.

"Open the door this moment or you will find yourself swinging by first light!" the voice boomed again.

"That's James, the king's brother," Zoe suddenly said. "What can he want at such a late hour?"

I heard the bolts slide across the door, then swing open. But my friends still looked like half-wolves, and hadn't the preacher said that the king had no idea of who or what they truly were? Yet in an instant they once again looked their normal selves. Gone were their claws, vicious-looking teeth and wild hair.

How the fuck did they do that?

I could see a man standing just outside the front door. He was tall and wiry, with long brown curly hair that framed his pale face. Like the preacher, he had a moustache, but his was immaculately cut and trimmed into a neat line.

"Well, don't just stand there, Preacher," the man complained. "Invite me in to your home and out of this blasted cold."

The king's brother, James, emerged out of the cold shadows and into the room. I looked him up and down. I had never seen so many freaking frills in my life! He wore a mauve coat and white shirt underneath. The collar was a mass of white frilly material. The frills spilled down the front of him, and sprouted from the silky sleeves of his coat. On his legs he wore breeches and stockings. His shoes were black, square-toed and fastened with the gaudiest gold buckles I had ever seen.

Zoe looked at me as I stood agog. "I told you he was hot," she murmured behind her hand.

"He looks like he's just stepped out of a frigging Adam Ant video," I murmured back.

Zoe looked puzzled. "What's an Adam Ant video?"

"Doesn't matter," I said with a shake of my head.

Zoe cupped her hand around her mouth again and breathed, "Shame about his hair though."

"What's wrong with it apart from all the ringlets?" I asked.

"It's a wig."

"Get the fuck out of here," I choked, stifling the urge to laugh.

"Honest, I'm telling you the truth. Most of the rich guys wear them."

"And Harry?" I asked, trying to push the ridiculous image of him that had just appeared from my mind.

"Stamped on his wig, then set it on fire," Zoe giggled. "Refused to wear it. Said he wasn't going to look like a girl for anyone."

"Now, I would've liked to have seen that," I giggled back.

"And who might you be?" I heard a voice ask.

James had come to stand before me, chest puffed out. God, so many frills, I thought again, and tried to hide my smirk.

"Is something amusing you?" James asked.

"You'll have to forgive Samantha," the preacher said, coming forward. "She has only just arrived here."

"And where is it you hail from?" James asked, searching my face with his eyes.

"Whitechapel . . ." I started.

"Why, we are in Whitechapel," James pointed out.

"Woolwich," the preacher cut in. "She's from the village of Woolwich. She gets easily confused."

"A simpleton, you mean?" James raised an eyebrow.

"Hey!" I started.

"Just in awe of being in your presence," Harry said, taking me by the arm and guiding me away. Then, leaning in close, and out of earshot of the prince, he whispered in my ear, "Now keep your mouth shut and only speak when spoken to."

"You'd really like that, wouldn't you, you sexist pig," I hissed back, yanking my arm from his grip.

I skulked away from him, joining Louise on the other side of the room. The burning embers hissed, sending a shower of sparks up the chimney.

"Arrogant jerk," I muttered.

"That's Harry," Louise said indulgently. "You've got to love him."

I wasn't sure that I could love him, but I did want him, and that's what really pissed me off. We'd had sex on that train in '88, he must remember that. Didn't it mean anything to him? Knob-end!

"So to what do we owe the pleasure of your company at such an hour?" the preacher asked the prince.

"The king demands an audience with you," James told him.

"Tonight?" the preacher asked, and for the first time ever, I thought I saw the faintest spark of fear in his piercing blue eyes.

"Tonight," James said, walking briskly back across the room. At the door, he stopped and looked back at the preacher. "The king doesn't want to be kept waiting. And bring the monks with you."

He strode out into the night.

"Monks?" I spluttered. "I'm not a monk!"

Harry glowered at me. "That's a real shame, because you could have taken a vow of silence. Might have put an end to all your goddamn whining."

"I don't whine!" I snapped at his back as he disappeared out of the door after the prince.

9

The prince rode ahead of us in a black carriage. The horses which pulled it were black, as were the clothes the driver wore. Everything about it was black, apart from the gold crest of arms that was fixed to the doors on either side. The giant wheels clattered over the cobbled streets as we crossed London. We followed on horseback. Each of my friends had their own horse, apart from me. And it was as I climbed up behind Louise that I remembered the horse the preacher had given me in 1888. The animal had been beautiful, shimmering white in its coat of white fur. What had I named her? With that unreachable itch inside my brain, I leant close to Louise as she sat before me.

"What did I call my horse?"

"Which one?"

"The horse I had in the Old West – 1888?" What other horse could I have been talking about?

"Moon," she said.

"Moon." I smiled to myself. I could remember the name now. "What happened to her?"

"What do you mean?" Louise asked, her long dark hair fluttering against my cheek.

"Well, I got blown up in that mine, remember, so what happened to my horse, did one of you take care of her for me?"

"That was the day Zoe bit me," Louise said. "I'm sorry, I don't remember what happened to Moon."

"What do you remember?" I pushed, just wanting to discover more about my friends – more about Louise. I knew nothing about any of them.

"I went back – *shifted.*" She spoke low, as if telling me her deepest secret.

My heart skipped a beat. "What does that word mean? Please tell me." The sound of the horses' hooves clattering over the uneven streets was so loud that I feared I might not hear her answer. I wrapped my arms tight about her waist, pressing close against Louise's back.

"We shift through time, Sammy," she said, hooking a stray length of hair from the side of her face as the wind blew all about us.

"So you travel backwards and forwards through time too?" I needed to know. Louise had once been like me – just human – before she had been bitten by Zoe, so perhaps she went back to her own time just like I went back to 2014?

"Yes," she said. "I travel back too."

"Back to Colorado of 1888?" I asked. "That's where you started out, wasn't it? That's where you first met the preacher?"

"Look, Sammy, I don't have the answers you're searching for," she said over her shoulder at me.

"Then who does?"

Without saying a word, Louise stared at the preacher.

Knowing I would get little more information about shifting or anything else from Louise, I looked about me at the London of 1665. It was nothing like the London where I lived. The roads were narrower, it stank of shit if I was to be honest, and the houses were packed tight next to each other down dim little streets. This London made no noise. There was always noise in the London I knew. Even in the dead of night you could hear traffic, the whoop-whoop of cops' cars, ambulances and fire engines. The future was loud, not silent like the past seemed to be. If I listened really hard, I was sure I could make out the sound of water lapping against a shore. Could that be the River Thames? There was a part of me that would like to explore this London, but somehow I didn't think I would get the chance. But what was the point of time-travelling if I couldn't stop every now and then and take a look around? It would be like going on holiday to Paris and being locked in a hotel room. All you would see was what the view offered through the window. I had never been to Paris, but hoped to go one day.

In the distance, silhouetted against the night sky, I could see a tall spire. I didn't recognise it. No such building existed in the London I had come from. I pointed at it as Louise coaxed our horse forward by gently tugging on the reins.

"What's that building over there?"

"St Paul's Cathedral," she said.

I looked ahead again. "It can't be. St Paul's has a domed roof. Not a spire."

"That version of St Paul's Cathedral burns down next year during the Great Fire of London," Louise said. "It's redesigned and rebuilt by Christopher Wren. He rebuilds it with a domed roof – the version that exists where you come from."

"So if there had never been the Great Fire of London, then that building could still be standing today?" I tried to wrap my brain around the idea.

"Who knows." Louise shrugged. "History constantly changes things."

"Do we change history?" I asked.

"Sometimes." She made a clucking noise with her tongue, urging the horse into a slow trot.

I looked back at the spire of St Paul's, guessing that when I got back home to 2014 I would be the only person living who had seen the original cathedral. That was kinda freaky. As I looked up at the tower, I saw the milky blue rays of moonlight creep around the edges of the dark clouds that scudded across the night sky. My friends saw those rays too and quickly pulled their hoods up over their heads.

10

The preacher got his horse to canter and the others followed. It was as if they wanted to speed up, get out of the moonlight. But they dared not overtake the prince's carriage ahead of us. I glanced around to get my bearings. London seemed out of shape – out of time – yet some parts were still vaguely familiar to me. The ground beneath the horses' hooves had turned to gravel. Grass and trees stretched away from either side of us. I looked ahead and saw a huge cluster of buildings, or was it just the one building? A palace, perhaps. Some of it was constructed from white stone and pillars; other parts from a red fiery-coloured brick.

"What is that place up ahead?" I asked Louise.

"Whitehall Palace," she said back. "It's where the king lives."

Whitehall? Downing Street? Just like St Paul's, the palace looked different. But as I drew nearer, I thought perhaps I did recognise some of it. The giant arches at the front, and wide gravel path leading to it, was that Horse Guards Parade? The Mall? If so, we were now riding through St James's Park.

The prince's carriage rattled on; its huge black wheels threw up a fine spray of gravel that wound its way towards the imposing palace ahead of us. We followed, the horses at a steady canter, the wind blowing through my long blond hair. Like my friends had, I pulled my hood up, so it hung by the sides of my face. We reached the arch and I could see that it was guarded by men wearing long red coats and round metal hats. On seeing the prince's carriage they waved us through without any hindrance. We passed through one of the arches that supported the giant stone turrets above us. Torches were fixed to the walls, and their flames flickered in the whistling wind around the towering walls of the palace. The carriage clattered into a cobbled courtyard and stopped. The preacher eased back on the reins and his horse slowed to a halt. We drew alongside him, as did Harry and Zoe. Two grubby-looking boys appeared from the shadows and took hold of our horses' reins. After we had dismounted, the young boys led the horses away across the courtyard towards a stable. The horse which had drawn the prince's carriage neighed and pawed at the cobbles with its hooves.

A man wearing nearly as many frills as the prince

rushed forward, placing a box on the ground by the carriage. The door opened and the prince stepped out on to the box, then down on to the ground. The man who had brought out the box stayed bent forward at the waist until the prince was clear of the carriage and was striding away across the courtyard. With our hoods still up, we followed him over the straw-covered cobbles and into the palace.

The prince led us through what seemed like a labyrinth of passageways and wide corridors. The walls were covered in so many paintings that my head started to spin. Every wall seemed to have a face peering out of it at me. All of the portraits had those eyes that looked as if they were following me – watching every step I made. There were staircases too, that wound upwards and upwards until my calf muscles ached. What I would have done for a lift. Fine rugs covered the stone floors, the edges trimmed with gold thread. The interior of the palace seemed worlds away from the ramshackle houses I had seen crammed into the narrow streets on the other side of St James's Park. But why wouldn't it be different? This was a palace. This was where a king lived. And it was with that thought buzzing around in my head that the realisation of where I was and who I was about to meet struck me. I placed a hand over my mouth and released a short gasp. Harry glanced back at me, but his face was hidden in the shadows beneath his hood. He quickly looked away again. I was going to meet a king! King Charles the Second. What was he like? What did he look like? Why hadn't I paid more attention in history? Was he one of those kings that had gone around chopping off heads like King Henry the Eighth? Did King Charles like throwing people in the Tower? Were prisoners hung, drawn and quartered? No wonder the preacher had looked worried at the thought of antagonising him. I squeezed my eyes shut tight and tried to think of that sun-drenched beach and Harry packing out those trunks.

I opened my eyes to discover we had stopped before two white doors that towered high above us. Guards in red stood on either side of them. The prince pushed them open. I had expected to look into a long grand room, the king sitting at the far end on a blazing gold throne, a crown upon his head. Instead I saw a room that had one long wooden table running down the middle of it. The undecorated walls were made of a grey stone. A chandelier of candles hung overhead and lit the room. The king sat at the head of the table, a young woman to the right of him. His queen? They remained seated as James ushered us into the room, closing the doors behind us.

We stood in a line at the opposite end of the table, my heart racing before the king. Just like his brother, he had long dark hair that curled about his shoulders in tight ringlets. A wig? I wondered, willing away the growing smirk that threatened. He didn't wear a coat or jacket, just a white shirt that looked more like a frilly blouse. It was open at the throat, revealing a black V-shape of hair covering his chest. The king was clean-shaven, and had a large hooked nose and dark eyes. The woman to his right was pretty, with olive skin, dark eyes and hair braided into plaits on either side of her head. She wore a dress that was cut low, revealing her shoulders, with a string of pearls about her neck. Her dress was mauve and suited her dark complexion.

James went to the head of the table, where he stood next to his brother. With his back straight and a severe expression on his face, James looked down the length of the table at us. He really needed to lighten up. Then, in complete contrast to his young brother, the king eased his chair back, placing his booted feet up on the table, crossing them at the ankles. He plucked up a mug half-filled with beer and took a mouthful, his eyes never leaving the hooded preacher. After draining the mug, he smiled and said, "Anyone care for some beer?"

The preacher spoke softly in reply. "No, thank you, Majesty."

"Perhaps some tea then?" the king said. "It's very good. I never believed it would catch on. But it's become all the rage. Isn't that right?" he said, glancing to the woman seated at his right.

"Yes, Charles," she said, her voice meek but with a hint of a Portuguese accent.

"No, thank you, Majesty," the preacher said again.

I watched the King continue to stare at the preacher. Then, taking his feet off the table, King Charles stood and walked slowly down the length of the room. He stood before the preacher. "It's not like you to be so modest," the king said, staring into the shadows that obscured the preacher's face.

"Modest?" I heard the preacher say.

"It's almost as if you are trying to hide from me," the king said, tentatively raising a hand as if to unmask him.

I watched discreetly as the king went to remove the concealing hood from the preacher's face. What would he find beneath it? Had the moonlight started to change the preacher and the others? Would he discover a face that was half wolf and half man? If he discovered such an abomination in his palace, would the king have the preacher's head just like he feared?

Before the king's hands had a chance to do so, the Preacher pulled it back himself. I bit into my lower lip.

It was the man whose piercing eyes stared back at the king. "I was not trying to hide from you, Majesty. I was merely trying to keep warm. There is a chill wind in the air tonight."

The king met the preacher's gaze, a glint of mistrust in his eyes. Then, without warning, he worked his way amongst us, quickly pulling back all of our hoods. In turn, Harry's, Zoe's and Louise's faces were revealed. Stepping in front of me he paused, his hand hovering over my head. "Five," he observed, glancing along the line at the preacher. "You've added another to your flock?"

Before the preacher could make any kind of reply, the king had pulled back my hood. My eyes met his dark ones. I lowered my gaze. Then taking my chin gently between his thumb and forefinger, he raised my head, so I had to look at him. He looked as if he were studying my face. I could feel his breath against me, he was standing so close. Slowly, he drew his thumb over my lower lip, never taking his eyes from mine for a moment. My heart sped up. I couldn't help but feel the king's touch was inappropriate. Not because this was the first time he had ever laid eyes on me, but because his queen sat just feet away. I felt the ball of his thumb brush momentarily over the very tip of my tongue. He moved his thumb away and I could see it glistening in the candlelight with a daub of my saliva. The king raised his thumb to his mouth and mopped the drop of spit away with his lips, tasting me.

"I thought Christ's disciples were meant to be fishers of men?" the king said, speaking to the preacher but still looking down at me. "It seems every time you cast your net, Preacher, you catch yourself a beautiful mermaid."

Now I had been described by men as having a nice arse, big tits, and legs that went on forever, but never before had I been told I resembled a freaking mermaid. The king was smooth, but it wasn't that which surprised me. It was the fact that he didn't seem to care what he said in front of his wife. As he stood there assessing me, I couldn't help but feel my cheeks grow hot and my skin prickly. I looked away and it was then I met the queen's eyes. But she just looked meekly away as if she hadn't noticed her husband's behaviour.

With the atmosphere in the room growing more uncomfortable with every passing moment, I suddenly felt Harry at my side, taking my arm and steering me away. Was he doing that because he was jealous of how the king was looking at me – undressing me with his eyes – or was he worried I might open my mouth and say something I shouldn't?

"You forget, Majesty, that the preacher doesn't just catch young women in his net," Harry said, subtly pointing out the fact that he too followed the preacher.

"No, he catches himself one or two whelks too," James scoffed from the opposite end of the table.

Harry looked up at him, forcing a smile, when I sensed that if he wasn't the king's brother, Harry would happily have smashed his arrogant face in.

As if fearing the atmosphere might turn hostile, the preacher broke in and said, "Forgive me Majesty, but you still haven't explained why we are here."

"Because there has been another death," the king said.

"But there have been thousands over the last few months," the preacher said. "What makes this one so different that we are summoned by his Majesty at so late an hour?"

"The plague didn't kill the victim this time," James said.

"How can you be so sure?"

"Because the victim was eaten," a new voice put in.

We all turned to see a pale-faced woman step out of the shadows at the furthest reaches of the room.

11

How long she had been there in the shadows and who she was I had no idea. My friends didn't look as startled as I did so my first instinct was to presume they did know. She almost seemed to glide forward, the long pale-blue dress she was wearing trailing over the stone floor. Just like the queen, this woman was young with long dark hair, but hers was unbraided; it covered her shoulders and trailed down her back. Her eyes were as pale as her dress. Her mouth was small, but her lips were full, giving her face a slightly pinched look. She was very beautiful and in her mid-twenties, I guessed. She sidled up next to the king. The ease within which she stood so close to him suggested to me that they were more than mere acquaintances in his court, and very probably more than just friends. She seemed to be at ease in his company, an ease that only lovers really shared.

The king watched me watching her, a faint smile tugging at his lips. I could only begin to wonder what he might be imagining as he looked at both of us.

The king introduced us. “This is Lady Castlemaine.”

What did “Lady” exactly mean? Was that some kind of royal title? Did it mean I had to curtsy or something? I wasn’t sure, so I just nodded my head in acknowledgement of her. I glanced over at the queen, who still sat impassively at the table, her long slender hands folded in her lap.

“Eaten?” the preacher said, cocking an eyebrow at Lady Castlemaine.

James moved away from the end of the long table. “Don’t look so surprised, Preacher. This isn’t the first corpse we have found that looks as if it has been savaged by a pack of wild dogs.”

Zoe flinched beside me. Harry and the others stared impassively at the prince.

“My brother informs me that many a body has been brought to you with such mutilations,” the king said, eyeing the preacher with that look of mistrust I had seen earlier.

“That is correct.” the preacher acknowledged.

“So why then did you tell me it was safe for me and my court to return from my retreat in Salisbury?” the king asked. Not once taking his eyes from the preacher.

“I believed that the plague had retreated, that we had it under control—” the preacher started.

“It looks to me as if you have very little under control,”

James cut in. "The streets outside your church are littered with dead bodies. Why, when you should be burying the dead, are you digging them up?"

"The bodies are dead, but the plague inside them isn't," the preacher answered.

"Explain yourself," the king said. He seemed willing to listen to any explanation the preacher might have.

What reason would the preacher give for digging up the dead? I wondered.

He turned his attention back to the king. "The dead bodies are just hosts. The infection lives even though the flesh is dead. My fear is that as the bodies decompose they will infect the very earth. The earth that is burrowed by rabbits, foxes and rats. They will become infected again and in turn infect the population once again."

The preacher spoke with such conviction even I started to believe him, though I knew it was a lie he told the king. "The only way of truly ridding London of the plague is by burning the dead to ash," the preacher concluded.

The king's stare softened and a little of that mistrust melted in his eyes.

"So what of the mutilated corpses?" Lady Castlemaine asked, as if unable to let the preacher off the hook so easily. "Did the plague do that?"

"No," the preacher said. "I think the prince was right when he said they had been attacked by wild dogs. It would appear that I am just exhuming the dead and burning them."

"Just?" the prince spat.

"Don't you see, I was right? As the dead rot and fester in the mass graves, the stench of decomposing flesh is attracting animals. These animals are digging the dead up just like they would a bone and are being infected. They then turn on their masters, driven half mad by the plague, exactly like the rats did when they came ashore from the boats that had travelled here from foreign lands," the preacher explained.

God, he was good. But I guessed he was only really telling a half-lie. The stench coming from the decomposing bodies thrown into the mass graves was indeed attracting wild animals – the vampires.

The room had fallen into a sudden silence, and I could see that the prince was searching for a way to disprove what the preacher had said. But before he'd had a chance to say anything, the king spoke.

"So what do you suggest we do next, Preacher?"

"Get the dog catcher to round up all stray dogs and cats if need be," the preacher told him. "And we will continue digging and burning."

"And you call yourself a holy man?" James sneered, a look of revulsion on his face at the thought of the dead being exhumed.

The preacher looked at the prince with his cool stare and said, "Doesn't the Bible say that the living know that they will die; but the dead know nothing . . . their love, their hatred, and their envy have now perished."

"And what is that supposed to mean?" Lady Castlemaine asked.

"That the dead are already dead. I can't save them, but I can still save the living," the preacher said back.

The room fell into another hushed silence, and the queen sat alone at the table as if just a mere spectator to what was being played out before her. It was like she had no voice, or did she fear that she wouldn't be listened to? I often knew how that felt. It was as if Lady Castlemaine were the true queen as she stood at the king's side and questioned the preacher.

"I'll give you two more weeks to see if you are right in what you say, Preacher," the king said.

Then what? I felt like asking, but didn't dare.

As if able to read my thoughts, the king glanced at me, and added, "It would be such a pity to see such a pretty head skewered to the railings outside the Tower."

12

"You don't think the king meant what he said, do you?" I asked Harry as we crossed the courtyard in the direction of the stables.

Harry pulled the hood up over his head once again. "About what?" he grunted.

"About cutting off our heads and sticking them on spikes outside the Tower of London. I could imagine the prince doing it, but not the king. He seemed nicer . . ."

"Nice?" Harry gripped my arm and pulled me around to face him. "The king had Cromwell's corpse dug up, then had his head cut off! Do you think because you've got a nice pair of tits and blue eyes he might just spare you?"

Without giving me the chance to answer, Harry was away across the courtyard in pursuit of the others. Did he really think I had nice tits? Perhaps he was jealous of how the king had looked at me? Nah, perhaps not. Guys like Harry didn't get jealous. Guys like Harry didn't give a shit.

I followed Harry and the others, the half-moon peeking out from behind the clouds bathing the courtyard in a pool of blue light. The preacher had obviously been rattled by the king and the prince, for as I drew near he was arguing with the stable hand.

"What do you mean, we can't have our horses?" the preacher snarled.

"The horses do belong to the king. You were to only borrow them. And now the horses need re-shoeing," the young stableman said. His front teeth were brown and rotten, like they were smeared with chocolate. Straw stuck out from his dishevelled hair. He looked as if he had just woken up.

"Who says?" Harry barked at him.

"The stable head," was the answer.

"And where is he?" The preacher sounded more agitated than I could ever remember him sounding before.

"In bed," the stable hand said, picking the seat of his trousers from the crack in his arse. "He is not to be disturbed 'til morning."

The preacher took a deep breath. "So how do we get back to our church? It is late and our home is on the other side of the city."

"You can take that." The young man pointed one grubby

finger over the preacher's shoulder. We all turned to see a black carriage similar to the one that James had used earlier that night. The horse was sleek and strong-looking. "It's going spare and will do ya 'till the horses 'ave had their shoes done."

The preacher looked back at the stable hand.

"It's big 'nuff for all of ya," he said with a shrug.

In the distance, a bell chimed out twice, announcing that it was two in the morning. The preacher looked at the stable lad and said, "We'll take the carriage for now, but I'll be back for the horses."

The lad turned and went back into the stable where I suspected he would go back to sleep on the hay.

Within minutes we were clattering over the cobbled courtyard in the carriage. I sat up front with the preacher, Harry, Louise and Zoe tucked away in the carriage behind us. The preacher cracked the reins and the horse led us out beneath the giant white arches, past the guards in their blood-red coats, and out across St James's Park.

There had been room enough for me in the carriage, but I had chosen to sit with the preacher as I hoped to get some answers to the many questions I had. With his hood still up, as if sheltering from the moonlight, he produced two cigarettes from beneath his robes. He lit them both, handing one to me. I popped it into the corner of my mouth.

"Who is Lady Castlemaine?" I asked him. It wasn't the subject I really wanted to explore, but then again, I didn't want to hit the preacher with questions about shifting and why I found it so hard to remember anything. I thought it better to get the now-tetchy preacher talking first.

"She's the king's mistress," he said, looking straight ahead.

I had been right about them.

"Does the queen know?"

"Everyone knows," he said. "Lady Castlemaine's better known as the uncrowned queen. She has the king's ear."

"And his cock."

I heard the preacher chuckle. "I guess."

"No wonder the queen looked so unhappy," I said, picturing her sitting meekly at the end of the long table. "What's her name?"

"Catherine of Braganza," he told me. "Comes from Portugal. I don't think she is very well liked."

"Why not?" I asked, watching the end of his cigarette wink on and off in the dark.

"She's barren. Can't give the king an heir to the throne. But Lady Castlemaine has given him children. Three I think so far."

"Get the fuck out of here," I said, almost choking on a throat full of smoke. "You've got to be kidding me?"

The preacher shook his head. "Nope. They all live in that palace as one happy family. Or perhaps not so happy."

"If I were queen, I'd kick his arrogant arse . . ."

"We're not in 2014 now," the preacher reminded me.

Hearing him mention the time I had come from, I seized

the moment and said, "How many times have I travelled back? And why do I forget?"

"Duck," the preacher said.

I frowned. "Sorry?"

"Duck," he said again, this time pushing my head down with the flat of his hand.

I glanced back to see a hideous white face and set of claws lunging out of the darkness at me. The preacher's hand, now a claw, drove into the face of the vampire climbing up the side of the carriage. He dragged his giant claw down the length of the vampire's skin, removing its face like some kind of rubber mask. The vampire screeched, falling down beneath the wheels of the carriage. The carriage lurched from side to side as it rolled over the vampire below.

The preacher cracked the reins, the horse now dragging the carriage forward at a terrifying speed. It rocked and rolled and bounced over the uneven streets of London. I gripped the side of the seat, fearing that I might just be thrown clear and trampled beneath the horse's hooves or the carriage wheels.

"Get a grip, doll!" I heard someone urge me in my ear.

I saw Harry had broken through the roof of the carriage with his claws and was now perched on top. He had hold of my shoulder with one claw. I brushed it aside. Not because I was repulsed by it or his touch, but because I didn't need his help.

"I can take care of myself."

With his gums now full of jagged teeth, he snarled, "I'll remember that."

"Good!" I shot back.

The preacher's hood blew back, revealing his face. He too now looked more wolf than man, those white wispy lengths of hair billowing back from his face. He glanced sideways at me and gave a grim smile. He looked as if he was actually enjoying himself as he raced the carriage forward through the narrow smoke-filled streets of London.

Suddenly, the carriage rocked violently to the right, and I feared that the whole thing was going to spill over. I looked down to see more vampires climbing up the side. The rear of the carriage almost tipped back on its wheels as the vampires clambered on board. The preacher cracked the whip and roared at the horse as he fought to regain control of the carriage. The wheels scraped against the edge of the gutters, spraying up filth and dirt into the night air.

I looked back at Harry. He was holding on to the roof of the carriage as it lurched left and right. His now-long hair blew back off his face, revealing the thick bushy sideburns. He looked at me. I couldn't help but notice the same kind of grin I had seen on the preacher's face.

"You're actually enjoying this, aren't you?" I shouted over the sound of the clambering and screeching vampires.

"What's not to enjoy?" he roared as the preacher now raced the carriage alongside the bank of the River Thames.

Then in that moment, I was somewhere else. I was no longer on the carriage but in a car with Harry. We were tearing alongside another river, in another time and another place. I could see vampires clambering over the back of the car, their razor claws swiping through the night just inches from my face.

"The dagger!" Harry was bellowing at me. "The dagger!"

"What?" I said, blinking at him, feeling light-headed and woozy again.

"The stakes!" he shouted at me. "Get a stake!"

I blinked again, and was back on the carriage.

"Sammy, get a stake!" Harry was howling.

"What? Where?" It was like I had been in a very similar situation before.

"Samantha!" I heard the preacher yell. "Focus on here – focus on *now*!"

I looked at him, my brain swaying inside my skull as if punch-drunk.

"Not good," I heard Harry growl at the preacher. "She'd better not do that disappearing thing – not now. We're gonna need her tomorrow night."

"Tomorrow night?" I tried to say, my voice sounding thick and muffled.

I glanced up at Harry, my eyelids feeling heavy and just wanting to close. Over his shoulder I could see a tall structure. I tried to concentrate on it.

"She's fading!" Harry roared. "She's fucking going, Preacher!"

I fixed my sights on that tower looming up behind Harry. It rippled before me, going in and out of focus. I recognised it. Why could I see the Eiffel Tower? I was in London, not Paris. I'd never been to Paris.

"Stay with us, Sammy," I heard the preacher cry out.

The carriage lurched beneath me. I looked sideways at him. He rippled just like the Eiffel Tower had.

"Stay with us . . . stay with us!"

I looked up in the direction of the voice which was now shouting at me. A paramedic in green overalls. Leaning over me. Rocking back on his knees as he tried to reboot my heart.

"Stay with us Sammy," the paramedic said.

God, he was hot.

Commuters gawping over his shoulder at me as I lay on the platform.

"Stand clear!" he shouted at the gathering commuters. There was a whining sound like something electrical charging. He had what looked like two pads in his hands. He rubbed them together. "Stand clear!"

The paramedic placed the pads against my chest. I convulsed. Back arching off the platform.

"Stay with us, Sammy," he said.

Jesus, he looked like Harry.

"Come back!" I looked up at Harry and I could no longer see the Eiffel Tower looming up behind him, but a pale-faced vampire, its mouth sliced open across its face from ear to ear. Within a beat of my rebooting heart I had snatched one of those pointed stakes from beneath my cloak and thrown it through the air like a giant dart. It buried itself in the forehead of the vampire standing on the roof of the carriage behind Harry so that it spun back through the air as if being yanked back by an invisible bungee rope.

"I think she's back!" Harry howled.

"Praise the Lord!" the preacher shouted in triumph, and snapped the reins. "Faster! Faster!" He laughed like a crazy.

"Am I back?"

Reaching out with his hand, Harry gently squeezed my right breast. "Did you feel that?"

"Yes," I said, slapping his hand away.

"Then you're back," he said with a half-smile.

"From where?" I hollered, the wind rushing all around us as we teetered on top of the carriage.

Without answering, Harry knelt down and shouted into the hole he had torn in the roof. "Any chance you two lazy cows might give us a hand. We're getting our arses whipped up here!"

Again the carriage crashed into the gutter, threatening to send us headlong into a shit-swollen ditch.

Without warning the carriage doors flew open and away into the night, completely ripped from the hinges.

"You can't do that!" the preacher warned as Louise and Zoe sprang from within and climbed up on to the roof to join me and Harry. "This carriage belongs to the king.

He'll definitely have our heads off when we hand it back to him without any fucking doors or roof!"

Zoe and Louise both produced stakes from beneath their cloaks in a heartbeat.

The preacher worked the horse harder and harder as we raced on, the wheels screaming as he desperately fought to keep the carriage upright and on the road. Through the smoke that came from the fires burning across London, I saw more of those vampires speeding alongside the carriage. They sprang through the air, clinging to the sides with their claws. In a blaze of movement, Zoe and Louise had both thrown a volley of stakes at the vampires. Within moments they had reached beneath their cloaks and reloaded their fists.

"I love this," Zoe said, her eyes blazing brightly, pigtails rippling back over her shoulders. She threw several more fistloads of stakes in rapid succession. The vampires squealed like dying vermin as their bodies soon resembled something close to giant pin cushions.

"That's for my mum and dad," she screeched, as she rammed the pointed end of a stake into the upturned face of a vampire.

The vampire screamed as its face fell apart, its head disintegrating into a wisp of dust that blew away over the black choppy waters of the River Thames. Just like Harry and the preacher, I could see that Zoe was enjoying herself. The preacher steered the carriage on to a wider road, leaving the Thames behind us. He drove the horse and carriage on at breakneck speed, his piercing eyes fixed on the road ahead.

"There's more of those fuckers behind us," Louise roared, stake after stake flying from her fists like bullets.

"Where are they all coming from?" I shouted over their ear-piercing screams at the preacher. "I thought you said that there was only one!"

"Then I was wrong! It looks like we've got ourselves a nest."

"Not for much longer!" Harry howled, bounding over the roof of the carriage and dropping off the back.

I watched as Harry hung from the back of the carriage by one massive claw. I gasped, fearing that he might lose his footing and fall beneath the flashing wheels. As the vampires drew within his reach, he swiped at them with his free claw, slicing through their necks, their heads spilling back over their spouting necks and bouncing away up the street. Sensing the danger that Harry now posed them, several of the vampires changed their attack. They darted and scuttled over the fronts of the overhanging houses, dropping down once free of Harry. They now charged alongside us.

Seeing this, the preacher yanked on the reins, steering the carriage violently to the right, smashing the side of it into the fronts of houses and crushing the vampires flat. Houses began to fall apart in our wake, the right side of the carriage now nothing more than splinters.

"Now what will the king say?" Louise panted, leaning over the preacher and crushing her lips over his.

I couldn't believe what I was seeing. All of this mayhem and violence wasn't just exciting Louise, it was fucking turning her on. Smiling, the preacher eased her off him. "I need to keep my eyes on the road right now. Later, okay."

"Later," she repeated into his face, then ran her tongue over it.

Licking her lips, she reached beneath her cloak, produced a stake and buried it into the face of the nearest vampire. "Oh, yeah," she breathed, shuddering with delight.

With Harry still clinging precariously from the back of the carriage, ripping and clawing at anything that got too close, I stood on top with Louise and Zoe as we threw the last of our stakes into the remaining vampires.

With them crumbling to ash beneath the wheels of the battered carriage and tiring horse, we limped back towards the church. It was still dark when we arrived, and the preacher guided the carriage to the small stables at the rear. Working as a team, we unfastened the horse and led it into one of the stalls. The preacher, with hands on hips, stood and appraised the damage to the carriage by flickering torchlight.

"How we explain the damage away to the king, I do not know," he said with concern.

"Can't you say that one of the wheels got stuck in a rut or something and we had a crash," Zoe chirped up.

"A crash?" the preacher said, raising his eyebrows at her. "It looks like we fed the thing through a fucking wood chipper."

With the preacher and the others now looking like their human selves, I said, “So why so many vampires? Where did they come from?”

The preacher looked away from the wrecked carriage at me. “I fear that a vampire nest has taken root. Things are more desperate than I thought.”

“Well they won’t be troubling us anymore,” Zoe said with an air of confidence.

“They’ll be others,” Louise warned her young friend.

“Why attack us?” I asked.

“Why do you think?” Harry grunted at me.

“What I mean is, how did those vampires know you are all Skinturners?” I said. “It could’ve just been a random attack.”

“I doubt it,” the preacher said. “But let’s hope you’re right, because for the next day or so you’re gonna be on your own, Sammy.”

PART TWO
Watchman

13

The Pale Liege knew their time had come.

The humans above were sick. Very sick. A plague had come to them from afar, brought to their shores and to one of their greatest cities by an army of black bristling creatures. Just like his own kind, they had razor-sharp teeth, claws and preferred the darkness to the light. They carried with them an illness that weakened the humans, made them sick, and killed them in great numbers. The Pale Liege could sense the humans' growing frailty and fear. And in their desperation to quell the spread of this disease they dug great pits in the ground and threw their dead into them.

But these corpses were fresh dead, the blood was still hot and the flesh still warm. When the pits were filled in, the Pale Liege and his kind crept up from the tunnels and underground caves, digging upwards into the earth with their claws and taking the newly dead back down into the murky depths. It was here – it was now – that for the first time they tasted warm human flesh. And their Pale Liege hadn't been wrong – warm human flesh was so sweet. It was addictive and they wanted more. There seemed to be an unending supply of warm bodies as the humans filled more giant pits with their dead. No longer did the creatures have to survive on the cold flesh they scavenged, no longer did they have to turn on each other to fill their aching bellies. And as they ate, they grew stronger and so did their confidence in adventuring above ground. Their taste for human flesh and blood was ever-growing. How much sweeter would the blood and flesh taste if the human were not just warm but still alive when the first bite was taken?

The Pale Liege had a vague memory of such a delight but he had been beaten – defeated by his enemy, the Skinturner. And he now feared that his enemy might just beat him again. The warm flesh was growing scarcer each day. At first the Liege thought that perhaps the humans had found a cure for the plague that ravaged them. But this was not so. The bodies were being dug up, stolen back out from those giant death pits. It seemed that his enemy was taking back that flesh his kind had become addicted to. His enemy was stealing the very food from his subjects' mouths, just as they were beginning to grow stronger and the humans weaker.

Perhaps the humans had found a cure after all? Perhaps they had found the Skinturner? The Skinturner who loved the humans – who had taken it upon himself to protect them – to become their saviour. So the Pale Liege decided to send one of his own above ground to investigate, to infiltrate the human world. He sent the one vampire he trusted most: the Watchman.

14

I had no idea what time it was, but it was still dark. The others had gone to bed. I hadn't been able to sleep. The sounds of the preacher's and Louise's fucking was so loud I wondered how Harry and Zoe managed to get any sleep at all. My friend Sally and her cop boyfriends had nothing on the preacher and Louise. They didn't just moan and groan with joy, they nearly screamed the place down. I was surprised the whole of freaking London couldn't hear them. And it wasn't only the shrieking and panting, it was the crash and the thump of furniture being upturned and thrown about the place. Christ only knew what those two got up to.

When I thought I couldn't take anymore, their sex noises stopped. As I lay on my bed in the dark, trying to pretend that I wasn't just a little bit jealous that Louise was having all the fun, I heard the sound of a bedroom door creak open. This was followed by the sound of muffled voices. I heard the preacher whispering, followed by the sound of Louise giggling. Pulling a sheet from off my bed, I threw it about my naked shoulders and went to my bedroom door, opening it just enough to peer out on to the tiny landing at the top of the stairs. Amongst the shadows, I could just make out the preacher leading Louise down the staircase.

What were they up to? I wondered. They were like a couple of newly dating teenagers. At least someone was having a good time. I glanced along the landing in the direction of Harry's room, then closed the door of my poky room and went to the window. I looked out and could see the stables. From below I heard a sound, like a door being opened. Suddenly, the preacher and Louise appeared. Even though it was dark, I could see that they were both naked. I covered my eyes with my hands. It didn't feel right to spy on them. Louise giggled again. Slowly, very slowly, I opened my fingers and took a peek. I snapped them closed again at the sight of the preacher's pale body, before taking yet another peek. I had no real idea how old the preacher was, perhaps his white moustache made him look older than his true age. But his body was lean and muscular and his cock swung between his legs, long and firm-looking.

I really shouldn't have seen that.

More giggling from below.

My heart raced. Stomach knotted with a perverse kind of pleasure.

I could clearly see Louise now. Just like the preacher, her body was firm and toned. Her stomach was flat, her breasts large but pert. She had a small waist but strong-looking hips. They kissed.

I felt myself growing hot. To my shame I was becoming turned on. I imagined Harry leading me naked out into the night, to fuck me beneath the stars. To watch the preacher and Louise below reminded me of how I felt when I dared to watch my first porno. It had been one of Sally's. She had been at uni. I had sneaked into her room and taken it to watch alone in my room on my laptop. I had kept my bedroom door slightly ajar so I could hear if she came back early. I kept checking my watch while a feverish excitement rushed over me as I'd watched those strangers fuck. Those same jittery feelings rushed over me now as I spied on the preacher and Louise.

He slid his hand down the length of her smooth back, gripping her arse with one hand, cupping one of her breasts with the other.

I closed my eyes.

Heart racing.

Turning wet.

I shouldn't be watching.

I took another peek.

The preacher was leading Louise towards the stables,

one arm about her narrow waist. Was he going to fuck her in the stables?

I watched them go inside and close the door.

"Don't you know it's rude to spy on friends?" a voice whispered in my ear.

My heart leapt into my throat and I spun around, the sheet falling from my shoulders and pooling at my feet. Harry stood before me. He was stripped to the waist, wearing only trousers. With my heart racing, cheeks flushed hot and just wanting some of what Louise, Sally and everyone else seemed to be getting, I lunged at him.

Wind rattled against the windows as we clawed at each other. I fumbled at the buttons which held his trousers in place. With his help, I pulled them free. I raked my fingernails up Harry's back. I had never wanted any man so much. With images of the preacher and Louise and those strangers fucking in that porno movie racing through my mind and the sounds of Sally shagging ringing in my ears, I kissed Harry. Blindly, we staggered towards the bed. I felt so turned on I thought I might just burst without him even touching me. We fell on to the bed. I pressed my tongue against his, to the roof of his mouth, exploring his tongue with my own. From outside I heard the faint sounds of the preacher and Louise fucking again. This only heightened my own overwhelming desire. I'd wanted Harry ever since I'd arrived back in this godforsaken place and deep down, however much he tried not to show it, I knew he wanted me too. The smile I had seen play on his lips when he had seen me again had told me that.

With Harry now leaning over me as I lay naked on the bed, I arched my back, drawing my knees up so he could get at me. Harry sank down between my thighs. He wasted no time in running the length of his smooth tongue gently over me. I wriggled my hips with pleasure, losing my hands in his messy hair. Easing his face down, I raised my hips. I wanted more. As if sensing my growing desire, Harry slipped his hands beneath me. He drew me against his mouth and worked his tongue.

I tilted my head back, eyes closed. "Keep doing that. Don't stop. Not ever." If this was a fantasy and I was dying on an Underground platform, then let death take me if this was what it had to offer. I could happily die knowing that Harry was going to do this to me for an eternity.

Harry moved his tongue in a slow, circular motion. The sensation created deep within me made my stomach muscles clench. I pushed my hips into the mattress and urged him on.

"That feels so fucking good," I sighed, making fists with my hands, gripping the sheets. I gently moved my hips, enjoying the tingling stir between my legs that his tongue created. My stomach began to knot with an ever-growing sense of unbearable pleasure. The muffled sounds of the preacher and Louise fucking in the stables made me feel all the dirtier. I couldn't remember ever feeling like this before and I relished these new feelings deep within me.

Just like I had peeked at my friends, I now half opened

my eyes and looked down the length of my body where Harry knelt between my legs. I wanted to see if he was as turned on as I was. I wasn't disappointed by what I saw and the sight of his solid cock only added to my own brimming excitement. I closed my eyes, then shuddered, suddenly feeling his hands about my throat. To feel them there reminded me of the sex we had shared on the train in '88. Back then, Harry had taken me from behind, holding my head down so I couldn't look back at him. Knowing I couldn't was as good as being blindfolded and that had turned me on too. I kept my eyes shut tight now, wanting – needing – to feel those feelings Harry had once stirred in me. To be with Harry made me feel like a different woman. Being in the company of the preacher and the team made me feel different too. When I travelled back and spent time with my new friends I felt like a completely fresh Sammy, a more exciting one – the Sammy I wished I could be in my normal everyday life. So here I didn't really care if I gave myself up too readily to Harry. Here I didn't care if I stole a glimpse of my naked friends. Because I wanted to make the most of this fantasy, if that was what it was. I wanted to experience all the things I would be too scared to feel and do in my real life. Back home I felt guilty – like some sex fiend – for watching one of Sally's mucky films. When I was with the preacher and the team, I was Samantha Carter the cowgirl, the watchman, the lover, the adventurer, the vampire seeker. With them, I could be anything I wanted to be without consequence – without being judged. Who wouldn't want a fantasy like that?

So I eased Harry from between my thighs and brought his face up to mine. Cheek to cheek, I whispered in his ear. "I want you to fuck me. Just like you did on the train."

"You remember that?" he whispered back, with a smile.

"How could I forget?" I rolled on to my front. "It was the best I've ever had."

Harry gripped my arse with both of his strong hands and pulled me up into a kneeling position on the bed. He covered me once more with his mouth and I shuddered from head to toe. He tightened his grip. Then he was deep inside me. I couldn't help but squirm before him as I felt his cock push in and out of me.

"Oh, yeah," I sighed. "Move slowly."

Doing as I asked, Harry rocked slowly back and forth behind me.

"Do you have any idea how good that feels?" I groaned, dropping my head forward and keeping my eyes shut.

Harry pushed himself deeper into me.

"Just like that. Keep doing it just like that."

There was a growing fiery heat deep inside of me, an intoxicating, heady feeling; I just didn't want it to stop. Harry started to move a little faster. With every passing moment his breathing quickened. He pushed himself deeper into me, his cock feeling hot inside of me, making me wet.

The swelling ache I could feel between my legs grew

stronger and throbbed until it became almost unbearable. My heart raced as I began to work my hips back and forth in time with Harry's building thrusts. I wanted more of him. Then that giddy, explosive fire suddenly unravelled. An unimaginable feeling of desire spread through me. It raced from my very core and down between my legs.

"I'm coming," I cried out. "I'm coming so fucking hard."

Harry gripped my thighs, as I rocked back and forth on my knees. He continued to drive himself deep inside of me.

"I'm gonna fuck you so bad," he growled in the back of his throat.

"Go on then," I urged him.

Harry bucked his solid hips back and forth. I threw my head back, hair spilling down between my shoulder blades. He lost his fists in it, yanking my head back as if riding me.

"Harder," I told him.

And Harry did until he suddenly shuddered violently behind me. He cried out, his voice deep and booming. I glanced back over my shoulder, wanting to see his face as he lost himself to me. The look of ecstasy etched across his face was so hot. With Harry's strokes growing slower, the throbbing between my legs began to fade.

Together we collapsed on the bed. Panting and our bodies shining with sweat, I rolled on to my side and Harry on to his back. We didn't talk. Once he had caught his breath, he sat up, swinging his legs over the side of the bed.

"Is that it?" I asked. "You're going now?"

"I need some sleep before tomorrow night," he said, his back to me.

"You can sleep in here with me," I told him.

"We wouldn't sleep, you'd just want to fuck," he said.

"Wouldn't you?" I asked, propping myself up on my elbow.

"Yes," he admitted as he stood up.

I looked at his perfectly sculpted arse. He plucked up his trousers from off the floor and put them on.

"Why did you come to my room tonight?" I asked him. Was sex all he wanted from me?

He turned to look at me. "I wanted to give you something."

"You certainly did that." I smiled at him.

Harry took something out of his trouser pocket and threw it down. "I wanted to give you that."

I took a deep breath. The rosary beads I had found in that church back in 1888 now lay amongst the crumpled bedclothes. When I picked them up the crucifix swung like a pendulum before my eyes.

"I thought I'd lost this," I breathed in wonder.

"You left them behind," Harry said.

I looked up at him. "Left them where?"

"In Paris," he said, leaning over me. He kissed me softly on the mouth. The kiss wasn't hard and desperate like the kisses we had shared before. It was soft, gentle, tender even, and showed he wanted more than just sex from me.

But then, without saying another word, Harry left the room.

"Paris?" I examined the rosary beads that swung from my fist. "I've never been to freaking Paris."

I took a cigarette from the handful the preacher had given to me. With the smoke dangling from between my lips, I wrapped myself in a sheet and went back to the window. I glanced out at the barn. There were no more sex noises coming from it. The sky was turning pink as a thin strip of dawn light crept over the plague-ridden city before me.

"Paris?" I said again, looking down at the rosary beads in my hand.

In the growing morning light I could see those bodies the preacher had dug up lining the streets outside. As the morning light grew brighter and stronger, I saw thin tendrils of smoke start to leak from them. It was like their dead flesh was beginning to smoulder. Then, as the first rays of sunlight poured over the nearby rooftops and fell upon the street, the corpses burst into seething flames. Some of them twitched and jerked as if momentarily coming back to life. But the flames consumed them, turning them into nothing but ash which floated away on the breeze like giant flakes of snow.

15

"Never have I seen someone so beautiful," the Watchman whispered in the young woman's ear. With her back to him, he untied the lace that held her nightdress in place. A baby stirred in an upstairs room then settled again.

"Maybe you should go," the young woman replied. "I should never have invited you in. You're meant to be a watchman after all. Both my father and mother have died of the plague. There is only me and my baby sister left. I could be infected."

"I'll take the risk," he said, his breath hot against her neck. "I'm sure you'll be worth it."

He eased her nightdress down over her shoulders, releasing her young subtle breasts. He reached round and cupped them in his smooth hands. She sighed, wriggling against him, so her nightdress slipped down over her hips and thighs to the floor. He pulled her close, so her warm soft flesh was against him.

The scent of her freshly soaped flesh was making him feel almost delirious. She shuddered and stepped out of her nightdress that lay about her ankles. He guided his hands over her breasts, over the flat of her tummy. Moonlight shone through the window, making her naked flesh look like alabaster. A horse neighed outside the window, the sound of hooves clopping against cobbles.

The Watchman turned the girl to face him. "So much beautiful flesh."

"Aren't you going to take off your clothes?" the girl asked shyly. "At least take back the hood so I can see your face properly for the first time."

"You don't want to see my face," the Watchman told her, easing her down on to the wooden floorboards.

"Yes, I do," she giggled nervously. "I've only ever seen it from afar in the moonlight. I want to know if you're as handsome as I suspect you to be."

The Watchman admired the way her naked flesh shone in the moonlight, ignoring what she had said. "Beautiful."

From the very first night she had appeared at the bedroom window and called out to him, he had wanted her. These young girls he had to watch over were so innocent, naive, and vulnerable. They hated being locked up in their homes for six weeks or more, waiting to see if the plague had taken hold of them like it had their families. It was unnatural. They got bored, they got lonely. So as the Watchman guarded their door they couldn't help themselves – they had to talk to him – for who else was there to talk to and break the monotony of their imprisonment? So their conversation soon turned from subjects like the weather and the plague to more flirtatious matters. It wasn't long before they asked to look upon his face. But he was careful not to reveal too much of what lay beneath the hood. Besides, the Watchman knew that a young girl's dreams – fantasies – would create what she could barely see in the shadows. Then as the Watchman stood in the wind and the rain, she would take pity on him. She would want to invite him in to warm and dry himself by the fire. Of course she couldn't do such a thing; it might spread the plague, it was forbidden. But those forbidden acts were so often the nicest, the ones that brought the most pleasure. The young girl knew that and the Watchman knew she did too. So he would do his duty and stand in the cold, the wind and the rain and protect her home. He became her protector – he became her saviour. He knew she watched him and he knew it wouldn't be long before she broke the rules and invited him inside.

The hooded man couldn't have been very much older than her, the young girl had told herself as she decided that she would invite him to warm himself by the fire. A few minutes wouldn't hurt. And who would know anyway? The people who hadn't fled London kept themselves to themselves these days for fear of catching the plague from their neighbour. There was very little gossip for once. So she had done so just like the Watchman knew she would.

And as she now stood before him, heart racing, she just wanted him to take back that hood. She was naked after all. It was the least he could do. The Watchman pulled her close, and felt her speeding heart. The smell of blood pumping through it was almost overpowering. He ran his tongue over his lips beneath the hood.

"Let's fuck on the floor," he said, pulling her down.

The young girl flinched. The atmosphere in the room seemed to have suddenly changed.

"Maybe this isn't such a good idea. We might wake my baby sister," she said, willing her to cry out so she had a reason to end this.

The Watchman forced her on to her back, gripping her wrists and pinning her to the floor.

She wriggled beneath him, her heart and breathing racing faster. The Watchman liked that.

"Please, stop," she shouted.

The baby began to wail from overhead. She felt relief. He would have to stop now so she could go and nurse her baby sister.

But instead he forced her legs apart with his knee and sank between them.

"Stop!" the young woman screamed, so loud she drowned out the cries of the baby.

She felt a sudden burning sensation between her legs as if being bitten. Reaching forward, she clawed at the

Watchman's hood. With eyes bulging white in their sockets, the young woman threw the hood back and looked upon the Watchman's face.

Unable to believe what she was seeing, the last words she whispered were, "You're not a man at all . . ."

The cries of the baby continued, but were soon drowned out by the sound of the Watchman eating. With an appetite yet to be sated, he stole upstairs where the crying eventually stopped.

With belly full at last, the Watchman left the house and hailed the black carriage that waited just out of sight at the end of the dead-infested street. Climbing inside, he closed the door and settled back into the darkness of the interior.

The driver yanked on the reins and the horse pulled the carriage out of the street and into the night.

16

The sound of scraping was like a blunt blade being dragged over dry bone, like a butcher working with ancient knives and meat cleavers. The flesh long since rotted from the bone, leaving only the maggot-infested skeleton.

Scrape! Scrape! Scraaaaaaaaape!

I covered my ears with my hands and rolled on to my side. The light was too bright and I screwed my eyes tight as the last remaining fragments of my sleep fluttered away like smouldering pieces of flesh in the breeze.

Scrape! Scrape! Scraaaaaaaaape!

"What the fuck is that noise?" I croaked, opening one eye and shutting it again almost at once. The daylight shining through the window into my room was far too bright. I pulled the sheet over my head, willing myself to seek out just a few more moments of sleep.

"Hey Sammy, it's time to wake up," Zoe said, coming into my room.

"I am awake," I groaned from beneath the sheet.

"You don't look very awake," she said.

"I'm talking aren't I?" I mumbled back at her.

"I've brought you some breakfast." I felt her sit on the edge of my bed. How could I refuse her? Zoe was always so kind and thoughtful to me.

I poked my head out and half opened my eyes. "What time is it?"

"Nearly four o'clock."

"In the afternoon?" How could I sleep for so long and still feel like a sack of shit?

"Yes." She nodded, offering me a tray with a bowl and cup on it.

"Shouldn't that be dinner then?" I yawned, sitting up. She handed me the tray and I rested it on my lap. The bowl was full of what looked like something close to wallpaper paste. I wrinkled my nose. "What's that?"

"Pottage," Zoe giggled, checking out my look of revulsion.

"Don't you mean porridge?" I said, prodding it with a finger.

"No it's called pottage," she corrected me.

"What the fuck is it?"

"Boiled grain," Zoe said.

"Yeah, well, thanks, but I think I'd rather have a bowl of the pink stuff."

"Pink stuff?"

I took a sip of the tea. It was very sweet. "You know that pink-coloured pulp we ate in the Old West."

"That was red beans mashed up with—"

"Yeah, don't remind me," I said. "That was gross too."

I took another sip of my tea, aware that Zoe was watching me. The sun coming in through the bedroom window formed what looked like a halo about her blond hair. She wore it in pigtails again, just like she always did. She was no longer wearing the cloak from the night before, but a pretty green dress that came down to her feet.

Scrape! Scrape! Scraaaaaaaaape!

"What is that noise?" I asked, putting the teacup down on the tray.

"The others are shovelling up the ash left from those vampires we dug up," Zoe said. "They've emptied the pit and are waiting for the next lot of bodies to arrive."

"Arrive?" I wondered.

"Those that have died overnight are brought here by cart," she explained.

"Who pulls the carts?" I was keen to know as much as I could about the London I now found myself in. How long was I going to be here? Days? Weeks? Months or even years?

"The watchmen bring them." She got up and went to the window where she looked out, her profile beautiful in the hazy light.

Something about that name sounded familiar. Something

I had perhaps picked up in my school history lessons? "Watchmen?"

"If someone dies of the plague, everybody in that household has to be locked inside for six weeks," Zoe began. "If they haven't fallen ill or died in that time, they are given a certificate of health by the doctor and allowed to leave again. The doors of the houses get marked with a red cross so people know there are sick inside. They usually have a guard placed outside the house – a watchman."

"And what do these watchmen look like?" I continued to probe.

"They all look different I guess." Zoe shrugged. "But you never really get to see their faces as they wear masks or have hoods pulled up over their heads so they don't catch the plague."

I sat thoughtfully on my bed, eyeing my revolting breakfast. There was something about what Zoe had told me that made the itch come back – the one just out of reach at the back of my skull.

"Can I say something?" she suddenly asked.

"Sure."

Checking that the others were still outside, she came back and sat next to me on the bed. She spoke in a low voice, as if talking about something that perhaps she shouldn't. "I'm sorry if I haven't been a very good friend to you."

I was a little taken aback by what she said. "What do you mean? You've been a perfect friend to me. You brought me breakfast didn't you?"

"I don't mean like that. I know you have lots of questions and I feel bad that I can't give you the answers you're seeking."

"Why can't you?" I asked.

"The preacher says I mustn't. None of us must," she said.

I wasn't sure I liked the reason she gave. Why would the preacher want to keep secrets – especially when those secrets involved me? "Doesn't the preacher trust me?"

She shook her head. "It's nothing like that."

"Why then?" I pushed.

"The preacher really cares for you," she said. "He cares about all of us. We're a family – a pack."

"Like a pack of wolves, you mean?"

She nodded.

"But I'm not a wolf, Zoe, so how do I fit into your pack?" I asked, part of me suddenly feeling like an outcast.

Zoe looked over at the window, then back at me. "I wish I could tell you more, Sammy, but I can't." She climbed from the bed. "I'll see you downstairs."

"If you truly are my friend answer me just one question?"

Zoe stopped at the door. "What's that?"

"Is any of this real? Are you, the preacher, Harry and Louise real?" I almost pleaded with her.

"If you really want us to be," Zoe said, then left the room.

17

What Zoe had meant by her cryptic answer, I didn't know. Perhaps my question had been just as obscure. After I had washed, then dressed in the cloak I had arrived in, I went to the window. Just like I had the night before, I spied down at my friends. This time, though, both the preacher and Louise were dressed and Harry was with them. Zoe had been right; they were scraping up the charred remains of the corpses I had seen burst into flames at dawn. So the preacher had been correct to believe the dead had been infected by a vampire or they wouldn't have burned as the rays of the rising sun had touched them.

But what of the vampires that had attacked us the night before? Was *I* right that it had been a random attack? And if there was a nest of them as the preacher suspected, had we killed all of them? I didn't know and I guessed the preacher didn't know either.

I watched Harry shovel up the last of the ashes. He was stripped to the waist and a trail of sweat glistened between his shoulder blades. The winter sunlight was now fading, although it wasn't that which made Harry sweat so much, but the huge fire that continued to burn in the grounds of the church. I saw Zoe come out from the stable, her arms full with lengths of black wood, and toss it on to the fire.

"Where did you get that wood?" I heard the preacher ask her.

"From off that carriage," she said.

"Not the carriage," the preacher groaned. "We've got to take that back to the king, you know."

"Well it's pretty messed up already," Zoe said. "I didn't think a few more pieces would matter."

"I don't believe what I'm hearing." The preacher shook his head. "I'm trying to get everything sorted for Sammy while we're away for the next couple of nights and here you are dismantling the king's property and throwing it into the fire."

Hearing the preacher mention again that they were going away, I remembered that I would be left alone. I wasn't sure I liked the idea, so I headed downstairs. The preacher and Zoe were still arguing when I came out from the house into the graveyard.

"Well it wasn't me who smashed the carriage into those houses," Zoe snapped.

"And it wasn't me who ripped the bloody doors off," the preacher came back at her.

Sensing they were being watched, the four of them all glanced up at once.

"Hey Sammy." Zoe greeted me, the quarrel with the preacher seemingly forgotten.

Harry simply nodded in my direction and went back to shovelling. Was that all the recognition I got after what had happened between us last night? I thought of how he'd kissed me before leaving my room. I was sure it had meant something. So why was he acting so aloof again? Well, two could play at that game. That was the last time I was going to sleep with him. Not that Harry hung around long enough to do any sleeping.

"Sleep well?" Louise asked with a wink and a smile.

"Did you?" I smiled back.

Her smile turned into a grin. I liked Louise. Although she was about ten years older than me, we were more alike than perhaps I first thought.

She placed the shovel she was holding against a nearby tree and went and stood next to her lover. I looked at the preacher. "You said something last night about me being left on my own for the next couple of nights. Where are you all going?"

"Come with me and I'll show you," he said, heading towards the house. I followed him inside, Zoe, Louise and Harry at my heels. We crossed the small living room, through the door and into the passageway concealed behind the door in the church. The preacher took a torch from a fixing on the wall. Once lit, he led us back down the passageway, the torch casting long eerie shadows all along it. We reached the door at the opposite end, but instead of going through it and into the church the preacher started down the set of stone steps I had seen the night before. The stairs spiralled away into the gloom like a twisted spine. It was so dark that it was as if it soaked up the torchlight. The walls seemed to close in all around me as we corkscrewed further and further below the ground. I suddenly felt claustrophobic, like the darkness was smothering me. I wanted to turn back, but couldn't. Even if my fear had gotten the better of me, I would have never squeezed past the others behind me in the tight confines of the stairwell we were descending.

At the bottom, the air seemed thinner somehow, and I took a shallow breath. The preacher didn't seem affected by it, as he lit a cigarette using the torch he held in his hand. The end of the cigarette glowed bright red in the near darkness. The smoke in the small confines of the crypt was pungent and choking. The preacher offered me a cigarette but I shook my head. Something scuttled over my foot. I flinched. There was a mewing sound, like a baby far off, then Harry was holding something up in the light of the torch.

"Don't be scared," he said. "It's just a rat."

A sleek black rat bristled in his huge fist, its tail, long and grey, lashing from side to side. The rat squealed as he crushed it in his fist. The sound of its bones crunching and snapping made my stomach lurch.

"You're so gross," I said, averting my eyes.

"Don't want to be bitten by it," he said, throwing the limp rat away into the darkness. "Could be infected."

"Like your brain," I sighed, following the preacher.

I heard Zoe snigger in the dark.

The preacher held the torch above his head as he went into what looked like a small crypt. He cast the torch around so I got snapshot images of the dingy and dank surroundings. The walls were black and grey with grime. The only colour on them was the green moss and white mildew that covered them in giant patches. As we moved further in I could hear the drip-drip sound of water. The underground space stank of decay and rot.

"What is this place?" I said, too scared to speak above a whisper for fear of the ancient crypt collapsing and suffocating me to death.

"Where you will keep us imprisoned for the next two nights," the preacher said, appearing out of the gloom, our faces just inches apart. The flames from the torch lit up his glass-like eyes as he stared at me. "There is a full moon tonight. It will pass in two. You must lock us in here and not let us out."

"Is this what Marley—" I started.

"Shhh," the preacher hissed into my face. I felt the others gather around me, as if closing me in. It was I who now felt like a prisoner. "Don't talk, just listen, this is very important and your life will depend on it as will ours. Once you have secured us down here, you don't release us for any reason."

I could suddenly think of lots of reasons why it might be to my advantage to let my friends free. Fire? Flood? My own impending death at the hands of vampires? "But—" I started.

"No, Samantha!" the preacher boomed and I was sure I felt the walls shake all around me. "You do not release us until the full moon has passed. It doesn't matter what we say, what we promise you, you must resist. We will lie, deceive and try and trick you. But do not . . . *do not* believe a word we tell you until the full moon has passed. We will not be your friends – we will claim to be so – but we won't be, Sammy. We will hate you. We will want to rip the flesh from your body, we will want to torture you, hurt you in ways that you couldn't even begin to imagine."

I glanced sideways at Harry. He stared grimly out of the dark at me. I looked back at the preacher.

"Do you understand what I've told you, Sammy?"

"Yes. What about food . . ."

"Do you understand?" he repeated, gripping my shoulder hard with his free hand.

I nodded.

"You don't care about us. We are nothing to you while we are down here. We are nothing but animals," he said.

"You're my friends."

"*No!*" he roared, his voice now rumbling like thunder

in the confines of the crypt. "If you let us out you are fucking dead! We all are!" Spit flew from his lips, his eyes blazing. "Like you said, Marley has gone. We depend on you to keep us locked away."

"What would you all have done if I hadn't come back?" I asked, fearing the answer.

"You don't want to know," Louise said.

"Yes, I do," I insisted.

"We go on a rampage," the preacher rasped, his face so close now I could feel the spit from his lips against my face. "We hunt in a pack. We kill then devour . . ."

"People?" Now I did not want to know that my friends were capable of killing innocent men and women. The thought of them doing so terrified me.

"Anyone we find," the preacher said, his eyes never leaving mine. "Women, men and children. We tear them apart. We can't be reasoned with – we are nothing more than murderous animals. We don't discriminate between the young and old. Flesh is flesh. Don't let it be your flesh, Sammy." The preacher saw the bulging fear in my eyes. "Scared?" he inquired slyly.

"Yes," I admitted.

"Good. That's the plan." He walked away with the torch leaving us in darkness.

The preacher and the rest of the gang sat at the table in the living room and ate a pile of raw steaks. The meat swam in a bloody pool of gravy. Red juices oozed from the meat, ran over their chins and smeared their fingers.

They ate like ravenous animals – as if none of them knew when they would get their next meal. When the preacher had finished the last of the lumps of raw meat, he lit a cigarette, dropping the match where it floated in the blood staining his plate. The others sat in silence around the table while the preacher recited a list of chores I had to do.

When he started to talk I feared that he was going to give me a pile of his dirty laundry to clean, a mop and brush to tidy the place up, but by the time he had finished I wished that those really were the kind of chores he'd had in mind. He explained that once it had grown dark, the watchman would come pulling the cart with the dead he had collected that day. After he was gone, I was to check the dead for any black tokens on their skin or other signs that they might be vampires. If I suspected that any of the corpses were, I was to stake them in the heart then burn them. The others I was to place out in the street so when the sun came up those that I'd missed would be burnt. He assured me it was the quickest way of dealing with the dead since, working on my own, I wouldn't get time to stake all of the corpses and burn them. He told me not to stray too far from the church at night – it would be my only protection from any vampire attack. He reminded me, as if I didn't already know, that vampires would not be able to enter the church, and told me to lock myself inside it should any vampires come. Nor should I invite any strangers into the house. Vampires couldn't come inside unless invited. And on no account was I tell anyone where my friends were.

"We are vulnerable locked away," the preacher explained. "If the Pale Liege found out where we were, he would come for us. He would kill us while imprisoned. Marley gave up our hiding place once, but she paid for her treachery with her life. Don't make the same mistake, Samantha."

Was that a threat? I wondered.

The preacher pushed back his chair and stood up. Looking down at his friends gathered around him he said, "Ready?"

Without saying anything they too stood. It was like watching the condemned readying themselves for execution. I wanted to say something to them, anything – even if it was just goodbye. But it sounded too final. I wished that I had just a few moments with Harry though I didn't exactly know why. There wasn't anything that I could think of saying to him. It was like my brain had gone numb with the prospect of what lay ahead for me over the next two days.

Silently, I followed my friends as they made their way back down the passageway and into the crypt. At the bottom of the stairs, the preacher handed me the torch and a long rusty-looking key. There was a screeching noise, like fingernails being scraped down a chalkboard. I raised the torch to see Harry closing a gate I hadn't noticed on my first journey down here. Constructed of thick metal bars, it filled the narrow entrance to the crypt.

I saw Zoe reach out and grab Louise's hand as she stood beside her. Louise gave Zoe's hand a comforting squeeze.

I slid the key into the lock and turned it to the right, making a clanking sound that echoed off the walls. However hard I tried not to, I couldn't help but take one last look at Harry. He was staring at me through the bars, his face impassive, unreadable. I turned away, but then back as a hand gripped my wrist. I looked back into Harry's eyes.

"Be safe," he said.

"I'll try," I promised, then left the crypt, gripping the key to my friends' prison tight in my fist.

18

I reached the top of the stone steps and looked back down into the darkness. It seemed to almost reach out for me, wanting to drag me into its gloomy cold depths. The silence below was now thick and deafening. How long it would remain like that I didn't know. It would be night soon, bringing with it the full moon that would change my friends. How could such a thing of beauty make monsters of them? But they weren't my friends over the next two days and nights; I had to keep reminding myself of that. Whatever happened I couldn't set them free. The preacher couldn't have instilled in me more than he had the dangers I faced should I unlock them. I looked at the key in my hand. It was all that stood between me and death until the full moon completed its cycle.

Pushing the key into one of my cloak pockets, I turned

away from the well of darkness and headed down the passageway, the flickering torch I was holding throwing my hooded shape up the walls around me. Once in the living room I closed the door behind me. For the first time since arriving in 1665, I felt totally alone. I had often felt alone in my life – in 2014 – but that was different. If it got too bad I could always go and watch some TV with Sally, have a cup of tea or two, smoke a pack of cigarettes while listening to her latest sexploits. Here the sudden loneliness I felt was all-consuming. I knew no one here other than the preacher and his gang. Without them I felt lost. As I stood and began to dread the next two days and nights, I heard a voice, distant and muffled. Was that one of my friends calling out to be freed already? God, I hoped not. Was the moon even up?

I went to the window and pulled the grubby curtain back. The view through the window didn't reveal much, just the swaying branches of the ancient trees in the graveyard. I went to the front door and swung it open. A shower of dead leaves fluttered past on the cold wind that was starting to pick up. The constant fire raged in the centre of the graveyard, gravestones lay smashed and the death pit empty. The preacher and the gang had burnt the last of the remaining bodies so until more were brought by cart, the graveyard looked bleak and haunting with its empty graves and mounds of earth. It seemed to me I had travelled back three hundred and forty-nine years to become a gravedigger.

The voice came again, and I realised it wasn't from the crypt beneath the church at all, but from further down the street. Slowly I made my way across the desolate graveyard, pulling my cloak tight about me in the blustery chill wind. At the gate of the graveyard, I peered down the street and into the darkness. There was a lone figure heading in my direction, guiding a horse that pulled a cart behind it.

"Bring out your dead!" the figure called. "Bring out your dead!"

No one ventured out on to Aldgate Street as the horse clopped towards me while I waited at the graveyard gate. The man called out just once more before reaching me. The smell of decomposing flesh wafted from the cart and I wished I had one of the pointed leather masks that the watchman was wearing.

"Where's the preacher?" the watchman asked from behind his mask, his voice sounding muffled.

I looked into the round black covered holes he had for eyes. He really did look like some kind of zombie Womble. I would never be able to watch that show again without having frigging nightmares. He wore a wide-brimmed hat on his head, a long brown coat and trousers that disappeared in a set of mud- and shit-splashed boots. Nice.

"The preacher?" the voice came again.

"Huh?" I looked up from his boots, covering my nose with my hand.

"Where is the preacher?"

"He's not here," I said.

"The others?"

I suspected he was referring to Harry, Louise and Zoe. "Not here either."

"Where 'ave they gone?"

Those black holes in the freaky-looking mask unnerved me; I couldn't see the eyes of the man I was speaking to. What could I say in answer to his question? Where did a preacher and a group of monks go when they fancied a night off? "They've gone on a pilgrimage," I said, plucking out the first thing that came to mind.

"For how long?" the watchman asked.

"Just a day or so," I told him, wondering what concern it was of his. "Is there a problem?"

"Not for me," he wheezed as if starting to chuckle. "For you."

"Say what?"

The watchman hooked his thumb in the direction of the cart the horse had been pulling. "I've got a whole load of dead for ya."

As if to prove the point, he went to the cart and pulled free the large sheet of tarpaulin that covered it. It flapped in the wind like a giant sail. I looked at the cart and placed my hands to my face, fighting back the scream that threatened in the back of my throat. A mountain of corpses lay tangled in a giant mass of arms, legs and heads. Hideous and contorted faces stared back at me, their eyes black and dead. The stench was gut-wrenching and I felt hot bile splash into my mouth. I clutched my stomach, bent forward and retched.

"You're new to this, ain't ya," I heard the watchman remark.

I nodded my head, arming away the vomit that now swung like a bungee rope from my chin. "Can you help me?" I asked. There was no way I was going to be able to drive stakes into the hearts of those dead people. Some of them I could see were children. I would do anything for the preacher, but I feared he had asked too much of me this time even though I knew he wanted me to check the bodies for the black tokens he spoke of. I glanced up at the mountain of dead, their white contorted limbs trailing over the sides of the cart, heads thrown back, each of their faces a frozen mask of agony for the rest of time.

My stomach began lurching once more. Then, from the corner of my eye I saw the huge fire that continued to burn in the centre of the graveyard. Surely if I burnt them, just emptied the cart full of bodies on to that fire, that would be good enough? What difference would it make if I staked their hearts or not? The fire would destroy any infection the vampires had left behind and stop it from spreading.

"Help you do what?" he asked, those black holes fixed on me.

"Could you lead the horse and cart into the graveyard and empty the bodies on to the fire?" I felt desperate for his help but did not want to sound too needy.

The watchman surveyed the scene: the putrefying bodies, the fire.

"Silver." He held out one gloved hand.

"Silver?" I breathed. "I don't have—"

"No silver, no help," he said, turning away and heading to the cart. He started to unfasten the back, threatening to spill the mountain of bodies into the street.

I didn't have any silver. I thrust my hands into the pockets of my cloak. My fingers brushed over the rosary beads Harry had given back to me. The cross which hung from the end was silver, but I didn't want to part with that. Then in my other pocket my fingers felt cold metal. The coins! The French francs I had discovered in the Underground Station. I had no idea where they had come from or who had given them to me. But whoever it had been, I now felt like kissing him. I took three from my pocket, leaving the rest. I might need them tomorrow night, should I require the watchman's help again.

"I have these," I said, holding out my hand.

The watchman came towards me. He looked down into my hand, made a grunting noise behind the mask and took the coins, then held them up in the firelight and inspected them. Would he accept French francs? Would he even know or care what they were? He closed his fist around them, placing them in the pocket of his shabby coat. I couldn't imagine how much he got paid to watch the dead and I guessed whatever the amount, it could never be enough.

"Do we have a deal?" I asked, watching him move towards the horse and cart.

He gripped the horse's reins. The dark-brown creature neighed and shook its head from side to side, its sandy-coloured mane and tail swishing to and fro. "Open the gate," the watchman said.

Feeling like I wanted to punch the air with joy, I opened the gate, which screamed on a set of rusty hinges. The watchman led the horse and cart into the graveyard towards the fire and I followed, my cloak flapping around me like a set of black wings. I bent low as the wind blew dead leaves and ash from the fire up into the air.

First he turned the horse so the back of the cart was facing the fire, then went and got the bolt open. At once the pile of bodies cascaded out and into the fire. Sparks flew up into the night sky as the corpses spilled over each other into the flames. The fire took hold of the dead's hair, clothes and flesh. That sweet but sickly smell of pork wafted through the air. It did little to mask the stench of death that emanated from the stack of festering corpses.

Some fell short and the watchman picked up one of the spades the gang had been using earlier that day. He pushed and shoved the bodies into the fire. More dropped short of the flames so, picking up another spade, I helped him. The last of the bodies thumped into the graveyard and rolled over. The watchman stopped shovelling, straightened up and placed his hands in the small of his back.

"I'm done," he said, locking the back of the cart.

There were still many dead bodies on the ground that had yet to be pushed into the fire. "But these bodies need to be—"

"You put any more on that fire right now and you'll smother the flames out," the watchman said. "You'll have to wait a few hours or so. And by that time I'll be in me bed."

I sighed, looking aghast at the remaining corpses scattered about the graveyard. It was then I saw something that almost stopped my heart. One body stood out from all the others. There wasn't much left of it, but from what little of the flesh and bone I could see, it was female and her one remaining breast was covered in bite marks. "Hang on!" I called out after the watchman.

"What now?"

"This body," I said, pointing down at the fleshless remains.

"What about it?"

I looked up at him. "It looks like she was eaten."

"Dogs probably got to 'er before I did." The watchman shrugged, turning his back to me again.

"Where did you find this body?" I yelled after him over the sound of the swaying branches overhead.

"On Dock Street," he shouted over his shoulder.

"Where exactly?"

"Number three." Then he was gone, leading his horse and cart away into the night. I looked down at the remains and couldn't help but think of what the preacher had said about bodies being eaten by dogs. That's what he had told the king, but he hadn't really believed dogs were the culprits, he just said that to buy himself some more time. The preacher believed the dead were being eaten by vampires.

Alone in the graveyard, I pulled my cloak tight about me as the moon shone out from behind the clouds. It was blue, fat and round. From beneath the ground, I was sure I could hear the sound of creatures howling.

19

Not wanting to stay and listen to the growing, desperate howls of my imprisoned friends, nor wanting to hang out at the graveyard until I could pile more of the dead on to the fire, I made for the stables at the back of the church. What little was left of the king's carriage stood to one side. It was slowly being covered in white ash that blew through the night from the fire. I went to fetch the horse from the stable and rode it out into the graveyard. The watchman said that it would be a few hours before I could add any more of the bodies to the fire without fear of smothering it. He had also said that he'd discovered the half-eaten body at number three Dock Street. I knew Dock Street. If it was the same as the one in 2014, then it wasn't too far. The preacher had warned me against leaving the church, but I couldn't just sit here, waiting for the dead to burn. Gently prodding at the horse's sides with my boots, I headed in the direction of Dock Street and the house where the eaten remains of the body had been found. I wondered if going there might offer me some clue as to who had killed her. Or was I just kidding myself? Was I not simply just escaping the sounds of my friends howling and the sight and smell of all of those dead bodies? If I were to be honest, I was running away. I couldn't wait alone at that nightmarish graveyard, and I might learn something that could help me and my friends discover the identity of the vampire we were searching for.

I rode the horse through the narrow streets. Each of them was filled with smoke so thick it was like a fog that swirled all around me. At regular intervals there was a street fire burning. The preacher had told me it was believed the smoke would rid the air of germs and therefore prevent the plague from spreading. Annoyed, he had told me it did nothing but give the vampires a cloak to hide behind.

Slowly I rode on. Sometimes it became so thick I could barely see more than just a few feet in front of me and I only passed a handful of people as I made my way down the murky, empty thoroughfares. Each of them shot me a quick stare then looked away again; they either wore a hanky pulled across their face like bandits, or a posy of garlic and herbs at their throat. I passed houses with candles that flickered in the windows. There were buildings with red crosses daubed on the front doors and men wearing hoods and masks keeping guard outside. Watchmen. They observed me go by, silent, not one of them so much as nodding an acknowledgement at me. An overwhelming sense of fear permeated the very streets I rode. It seeped from beneath those doors with the red crosses, from the gaps in the window frames of the houses where the candles burned and from those I saw as I passed. It seemed that fear had gripped the city of London and not the plague. But who could blame these people? They had seen thousands of their people die the most agonising of deaths. Friends and family had been set on fire or thrown into mass graves. Most people had fled and those few who had remained were either sick or dying or been denied entry into the surrounding villages and towns.

I rode into Dock Street, pulling my hood back just a little as I peered through the swirling smoke at the numbers on the doors. At number three I dismounted. The front door was ajar and a cross had been painted in red upon it. I looked left then right, but I couldn't see very far and the street looked deserted. There was a candle burning in the window of number five, but no red cross painted on that door. Lucky them, I thought, pushing open the door to house number three. In the narrow hallway rats scuttled away into the darkness beneath the stairs as I entered. There was a door to my right and I pushed it open. What little furnishing remained inside looked smashed and broken. Perhaps the house had been looted since the body of the woman had been taken by the watchman. A candlestick had been upturned on the floor.

I snatched it up and lit it with the matches I had in my pocket before going to the foot of the stairs. With the candle held out before me, I looked up into the wall of darkness.

"Hello," I called out. There was surely no one here. Perhaps I was hoping the sound of my own voice might drown out the sound of my thumping heart. I checked that the front door was still open just as I had left it, the horse standing in the street outside. Then I started up the stairs. The stubby planks of wood creaked beneath my feet and I trod carefully. At the top I found myself on a small landing. As I cast the candlelight around I could see three doors. One was open, so I tiptoed towards it, my breathing shallow and harsh-sounding in the silence. I looked around the edge of the door, covering my nose and mouth to stifle the smell and my scream. Just like the graveyard, the room stank. In the centre of it, covering the rough-looking floorboards, were the remains of the young woman that the watchman had failed to gather up. Rats gnawed at the red bloody pulp that was left. My hand holding the candle shook with horror and in its flickering blaze I saw the dried blood that covered the walls. The room looked like some kind of slaughterhouse. I turned back and leant against the wall. That young woman hadn't been eaten by any dogs, however wild they might have been. She had been ripped to pieces by something far bigger, something furious. I had seen pictures of crime scenes while studying for my degree in criminology, but nothing like what I now faced. Swallowing hard, and forcing down the bile that threatened to rise, I staggered out of the room and on to the landing. Then from downstairs I heard movement, like someone was walking around down there.

With the candle in my hand I made my way to the top of the stairs. A shadow passed across the wall in the hallway below so I snuffed out my candle, throwing myself into darkness. Placing one foot in front of the other, careful not to make the stairs creak, I inched downwards in the dark. Halfway there I could see the front door was still open. The horse stood whinnying in the drifting smoke. If I was quick, I could run down the rest of the stairs and out into the street and mount the horse before being discovered. I placed the candle on the stair before me, took a deep breath and ran for it. Reaching the bottom, I raced along the hall to the door. But before reaching it, I was grabbed from behind.

20

"There is nothing left to take!" the voice hissed angrily in my ear.

I spun around, yanking my arm free from whoever had grabbed me, and looked into the wizened face of an old man. His long grey hair, no wig, hung in wispy strips to the sides of his ancient face. He wore an angry snarl and I could see that his grey gums were toothless. He definitely hadn't been responsible for eating the young woman.

"They've already been and taken everything," he shouted, his breath smelling nearly as bad as the dead waiting to be burnt in the graveyard.

I recoiled, covering my nose with my hand again. "Who has?" I asked him, stepping back towards the door and the street outside.

"The thieves!" he cackled, his throat sounding as if it

were full of snot. Was this the onset of the plague, I wondered? I pulled the hood further over my head, hoping that it might offer me some kind of protection. What I really needed was one of those freaky-looking Womble masks.

"What thieves?" I asked, backing further away from him as he closed the gap between us in the hallway.

"They called themselves neighbours, friends, but they couldn't wait to get in here and steal all that was left. They are no better than the rats," he seethed.

"Were you her friend?" I asked, now out in the street. The air no better.

"Neighbour, I was," he said, hooking his thumb in the direction of number five. "Knew her father and mother before they died. Watched that girl grow up since she was knee high."

I couldn't help notice how his eyes glistened as he spoke of the girl and her family. "I wasn't stealing," I tried to assure him. For some reason I didn't want him to think I was like the others.

"What were you doing then?" he snapped with mistrust. Then eyeing me, he quickly added, "Do you work for him?"

"For who?"

"The king," he said, dropping his voice low.

"What makes you think I work for the king?"

He looked in both directions along the street and into the billowing smoke before saying, "I saw one of the king's carriages out here the night before last. I saw someone climb into it and they were dressed in a long black cloak just like you."

"I don't work for the king," I assured him, wondering at once why one of the king's carriages or men would be in a rat-infested part of town such as this.

"Well, whoever you might be, there ain't nuffin' left to steal, it's all gone already," he said, starting to shuffle back towards his house.

Seizing my chance to make good my escape, I mounted my horse, and yanked on the reins. Then I called after him. "What makes you think it was one of the king's carriages you saw the other night? There must be hundreds of such carriages in London."

From his half-open front door he looked up at me. "The carriage was different from the others."

"How?" I asked.

"It had the king's coat of arms in gold on the carriage doors," he said, before disappearing inside altogether.

I made my way back in the direction from which I had come. Why would the king come to such a place? What reason could there be? But the old man had said he had seen one of the king's carriages, not the king himself. He had spoken of a person wearing a long black hooded cloak. Why would the king conceal his identity? I suspected the king was something close to a perv when it came to women, but would he have started a relationship with a young peasant girl? It would account for why he would want to travel to see her in secret. I shook my head. What was I thinking of. I couldn't go around thinking that the king of England was a vampire. It was absurd. Ridiculous! If I was going to point the finger at the king then I might as well point the finger at myself. My own clothes were identical to those of the person seen leaving that house and I had one of the king's carriages sitting in the stable at the back of the church. Okay, so it was pretty beat up, but I still had access to one. If we had been lent one of the king's carriages then what's to say that another hadn't been borrowed by someone else? Anyone in the king's court could have taken one. Still, knowing that the vampire the preacher and the gang were searching for was likely someone close to the king was a huge step forward. My friends needed to know. But how? I wasn't to have any contact with them for the next two nights and days. Would they be in any fit state to comprehend what it was I was telling them, even if I did dare to venture down into the crypt?

I reached the church and crossed the graveyard. Glancing over at the fire I could see that the bodies I had earlier piled into it were now nothing more than ash. There was room for me to shovel on the remaining bodies. I secured the horse in the stable and gathered hay together for it to eat. After patting its muzzle, I went back out to the fire. The full moon was now high in the sky. I looked up at it, its milky blue rays shining down on my upturned face. As I stood before the crackling flames, I thought I heard the sound of an approaching storm. If rain came with it the fire would be at risk of going out and I had more dead to burn. But as I listened, I realised it wasn't the distant rumble of thunder but the howling of my friends locked in the crypt below, and more than that. It sounded as if they were trying to smash their way out.

I snapped my head forward and looked down at the ash-covered ground. Not because of the howling I could hear, but because a cold clammy hand had just taken hold of my ankle.

21

Screaming, I stumbled backwards at the sight of the white hand pulling at my foot. With my arms flailing wildly on either side of me, I fell on to the pile of corpses scattered around the fire. The ground suddenly felt as if it was moving, writhing slowly up and down. To my horror I could see that some of the dead were coming back to life.

Desperately, I tried to get up and away. But the hand around my ankle gripped tight. I looked down the length of my body to see the hand was connected to an arm, which was connected to the body of a hideous-looking vampire crawling towards me through the smoke and ash. I kicked out with my spare foot, driving the heel of my boot into the writhing, snarling creature's face. It screamed in pain, its voice terrifying and shrill.

"Get the fuck off me!" I screamed back, driving my foot into its face again. Now I really understood why the preacher had insisted I drove a stake through the corpses' hearts. Fire wasn't fast enough. I kicked out a third time, but the vampire refused to release its grip. I rolled over as the body twitched beneath me. Cold hands reached out of the mass of entangled bodies and snatched at me. Just feet away I could see a spade. I clawed my way forward, but the vampire that had hold of my ankle pulled me back again. With my eyes screwed shut, and the vampire's grip around my ankle threatening to break a few bones, I splayed my fingers out and fumbled for the spade that lay just out of reach.

So close to the ground, I could hear the wolves howling with rage. It was as if they sensed I was in danger but were unable to come to my rescue. If only I could get to them, unlock just one of them, they would be able to kill these vampires . . .

No! I heard the preacher scream in my ear.

What if I was able to release just Harry? He wouldn't hurt me, wolf or not.

He killed Marley, I heard Zoe now.

I realised that the vampire had taken hold of my shin.

The spade! I heard Louise guide me like some kind of older sister. *That is your way out of this. Not us. Don't turn, Sammy, not like I have.*

Gritting my teeth, I made one huge lunge for the spade. My leg exploded with pain. My fingers brushed metal. I looked up to see the spade was within reach so I curled my fingers around it and lifted. I rolled on to my back, my body now floating on a sea of writhing and wakening bodies. Screaming, I raised the spade above my head and swung it down. There was a crunching sound, followed by a sickening squelch. I opened my eyes to see the spade buried in the crown of the vampire's head. It let go of my ankle with an ear-piercing screech. Scrambling to my feet, I took my chance and raced towards the church. As soon as I reached the wide set of double doors, I yanked them open. I looked back just once to see those corpses scattered about the fire drag themselves to their feet. They twitched and jerked, as if waking from a deep sleep. I could hear the sickening sound of their bones snapping back into place. They stood before the fire, the flames dancing behind them. With faces white, hair matted with flesh and blood, they then hastened across the graveyard towards me. I slammed the door shut, but not before seeing their wide grinning mouths crammed full of those razor-like teeth.

With shaking fingers, I slid the bolts closed as the vampires collided with the doors outside. The doors rattled in their frames, threatening to break inwards, the sounds of claws beating and scratching against them from the other side.

I pulled the rosary beads from my cloak pocket and hung them about my neck. The wolves howled from below, and somehow this seemed to excite the vampires' scratching and hissing outside. I heard a loud scuttling sound as they climbed the sides of the church, looking for any way in. I ran up the centre aisle as I heard claws scampering over the wooden roof above. Darting around the edge of the altar, I pulled open the secret door fixed into the wall behind it and headed into the passageway. I closed the door behind me and looked at the stairs which led down into the dark crypt.

"Sammy," I heard a voice howl from below. "Sammy, come and release us and we can save you."

My heart raced as I teetered on the top step.

"Let us free," I heard another of them snarl out of the darkness. "We can save you, Sammy."

I briefly closed my eyes and pictured the preacher looming out of the darkness, imploring me to not release them whatever might happen. Then I turned away from the sinking footwell of blackness and ran down the passageway to the living room. Once inside, with my back pressed flat against the door, I stood shaking. I sucked in mouthfuls of air. Over the sound of my hitching chest, I heard tapping. At first I couldn't figure out where it was coming from. I moved into the centre of the room. The noise came again. From my left. I jerked my head in the direction of the window. Someone was tapping against it from outside. I went over and took hold of the edge of the curtain. One, two, three. I yanked it open. A white face was pressed against the glass, eyes bulging red and bloodshot, ragged mouth open revealing a mass of finely pointed teeth.

"Invite me in," the vampire pleaded. "Invite me."

I jerked the curtain closed again to shut out that nightmarish face. The sound of scampering came from above, clawing and scratching at the front door, howling from below. I covered my ears, desperate to block out those terrifying sounds, and clambered up the stairs to my room. I kicked open the door with my foot and screamed. One of those vampires was at my window.

Tap! Tap! Tap!

"Invite me in," it pleaded. *"Invite me in!"*

"Never!" I roared, dragging the curtains across the window. I threw myself on to my bed, drawing my knees up to my chest. As I lay in the dark the vampires swarmed over the roof of the house, tapping against the windows and begging to be let in.

How long I lay there, trying to block out those sounds, I didn't know. Eventually the vampires' pleading turned to screams: not of frustration but agony. Slowly, I got up and went to the window. Making the smallest of gaps in the curtains, I dared to look out. It was dawn and the sun was slowly rising over the rooftops in the distance. In the graveyard the vampires who had tormented me all night long were now staggering blindly about as the first rays of morning sun made their dead flesh smoulder, then burst into seething flames.

With a cigarette in the corner of my mouth, I sat at

the window and watched the vampires burn to ash, just like the others I'd thrown into the fire with the help of the watchman. When the last of them was nothing but ash, I slipped out into the graveyard. Even though the sun was up, it was cold. With one of the spades I shovelled up the vampire ash, and tossed it into the fire. A knot of pain was exploding in the small of my back when I went back to the house where I collapsed, exhausted and in pain, on to my bed. The wolves were quiet now. Good, I thought.

I closed my eyes and pictured my friends in the crypt below, hiding in the darkness from the vampires. And in the darkness behind my eyes I saw all of them, just like I had on the train when I had first discovered they were wolves. I had been scared of them. I had been scared of Harry and now I could remember why. He had confessed to killing Marley. She had once been their watcher – just like I was. But why had Harry killed her if she had been their protector?

Because she had fallen in love with Harry.

Marley had wanted the man she had fallen in love with to bite her – to make her immortal – so they could never be parted. But Harry had said that a werewolf bite didn't bring immortality, only suffering and despair. So Marley had turned to the vampires. She had led the vampires to the preacher and his pack. That was the reason Harry had killed Marley, because she had betrayed them.

But perhaps it was more than that. Perhaps Harry killed

Marley because he realised that she was more in love with the idea of being immortal than she was with him. Either way, I knew in my heart that Harry had it in him to kill anyone if it meant his survival. Did that include me?

PART THREE

Fire

22

The Pale Liege sensed the humans were weakened. The one he had sent before him had done well. There was a nest in London readying itself to strike at the city's heart. Even his ancient enemy wasn't as strong as he first suspected. The Skinturners had needed to rest and hide when the full moon had come. Why did they care about the humans so much? If they didn't cower away on each full moon, then they could have taken the nest. But the Skinturners were fools. They knew they couldn't keep their murderous desires under control once they had changed, so they were willing to make themselves vulnerable to prevent themselves turning on the humans.

By the time the full moon had passed then the nest would be ready to fly – to take London and those remaining humans left within its walls. They would conquer England's greatest city. London would have a new king. It would have a new queen too if the woman who watched the Skinturners wanted true eternal life. In fact, regardless of whether she wanted it or not, she was going to have it. The new king intended to have her as his queen.

The Pale Liege's creatures were moving freely through the city of London now. They were even readying themselves to go further afield, into the villages and towns where there was some more warm flesh. They couldn't hide forever. The fact that London had been left virtually abandoned had weakened it, and had made it easier for the creatures. They had been able to sneak out of the darkness and feed on the men, women and children. They didn't need the leftovers that had been thrown into the pits. Their hunger was no longer satisfied by flesh that had putrefied; they wanted fresher meat and they had taken it. The one he had sent ahead had taken fresh flesh to the nest, where the younger ones had gorged themselves. It soon became an orgy and their thirst was not yet satisfied. Those in the nest rejoiced as he did as their hour grew near. Only the Skinturners could have stopped them but they would have had to find the nest first and it was too late for that.

The nest was about to fly free.

23

Bang! Bang! Bang!

It was dark and it reached out and touched me, just like the claws beseeching me through the bars. I jerked backwards. I mustn't let their claws touch me. If they did they might just take hold of me, drag me screaming towards the bars they so desperately wanted to break down. Four sets of eyes blazing like hot coals in the darkness. Each one of them fixed on me, boring into my skull, willing me to unlock them – release them – set them free.

"Let me free, Sammy," Zoe pleaded. But even though it was a face of a wolf that looked at me, I knew she was smiling. A long fleshy tongue hung from the corner of her gaping jaws. "I'll answer all of your questions," she promised me.

"You lie," I said, taking the key to their freedom from my pocket and clutching it to my chest.

The preacher, the leader of the pack, saw the glint of the key in my hand. It reflected like a twinkling star trapped in his eye. He came forward, wolf head set between two giant haunches. "She doesn't lie, Sammy. Why would she? Zoe is your friend. All of us are your friends. I could answer your questions too. I know the most about you. I have known you the longest, right from your very beginning. I can tell you so much."

"Like what?" I wanted to test him, to see if he was lying. I wanted to know if I could trust him enough to set him free.

"Mummy and Daddy," he said, bushy tail wagging from side to side.

"You never knew my parents," I snapped. "You lie too."

"We do know you, Sammy, we know everything about you," Louise said, suddenly showing herself at the bars. She paced back and forth like a caged tiger. But she was much bigger than a tiger or lion. All of them were so big and bristling with fur.

"You know nothing about me." I gripped the key.

"I know where you go back to but more importantly where you come from," Louise said, her voice soft. Like a dream.

"Where then? Tell me." My heart was so desperate to know.

"Let me out and I'll tell you," she said, her long whiskers

brushing against the bars. "You can trust me. I'm your friend."

"No," I said.

"I can tell you more than that," a voice said. "I can tell you what you really want to know, Sammy."

I glanced left, to see Harry at the bars of his prison. Unlike the others, he didn't look like a wolf. He hadn't turned.

"You want to know why you forget," he said, now smiling at me. He had such a beautiful smile when he bothered to do so. I felt hot tears on my cheeks and closed my eyes, brushing the tears away.

"Tell me then," I said. But Harry was no longer standing by the bars, dressed in his hooded cloak. He was kneeling over someone lying on the floor in his cell. Harry was wearing a green paramedic's uniform. He looked good in it.

"Come back!" he shouted at whoever was on the floor. He raised one fist and brought it hammering down on to the chest of the person in the shadows. "I won't let you go again!"

I inched closer to the bars, desperate to see who he was fighting to revive – who it was he feared was going to leave him again.

He brought his fist up once more. But instead of bringing it down on to the chest of his patient, he reached out through the bars and grabbed the key from my hand.

"Stand clear!"

I dropped to my knees and drove my fist into the floor of the crypt. Harry had tricked me. He had deceived me to get the key and now I was dead. Without looking up I could hear the key being slid into the lock on the cell door.

"No!" I roared, banging my fists into the ground.

No! No! No!

Bang! Bang! Bang!

The sound of banging woke me. I sat up on my bed. The last of the daylight was seeping around the edges of my curtains and bathing my room in a dirty grey. How long had I been asleep? All day? All week? All month?

Bang! Bang! Bang!

The sound was coming from below.

The preacher . . . Harry . . . had they all broken free while I had been sleeping? They were at the forefront of my mind as I swung my legs over the side of the bed. Had I been dreaming about them? If I had, the remnants of that dream were now fading fast as I armed away a thin line of dribble from the corner of my mouth.

Bang! Bang! Bang!

I stood up. The noise sounded too close to be coming from the passageway. I hobbled from my room, my ankle hurting every time I put my foot to the floor. The memories of the vampire from the night before raced back into my mind so clearly I had to glance down to make sure I wasn't dragging the creature down the stairs behind me.

Bang! Bang! Bang!

The noise came again. Someone was pounding against the door. Raking my fingers through my hair to get rid of the bed head, I went to the front door and fumbled it open. The prince stood outside and he looked pretty pissed off if I were to be honest. Had he seen the wreck of the carriage? I wondered. No, it was by the stable, so unless he had gone snooping for some reason, he wouldn't have seen it. I hoped the preacher was back above ground when that happened. There was no way I was going to take the blame for that.

"Well, don't just stand there, invite me in," James grumbled.

"Oh, I'm sorry," I said, stepping aside doing something between a bow and a curtsy. "Please come in."

James stepped past me into the house. He stood and looked about the room, his nose turned upwards. He really was a pompous knobhead. Shame I couldn't tell him that without fearing my head would be hacked off. He was dressed in an abundance of frills and gold buckles again. He had the wig on too. Was he bald underneath?

"To what do I owe this pleasure?"

He ignored my question and why not, every other fucker did around here. He surveyed the room again, as if looking for something. In his hand he carried what looked like a small trunk. "Where are the preacher and the others? I forget their names."

Did I lie again and say they had gone on a pilgrimage? No, the king wouldn't really accept that as an answer like the watchman had. After all, the preacher was meant to be sorting out the whole plague problem, not taking a holiday. "They're praying."

"Praying?" he eyed me with that look of suspicion I had seen him show the preacher.

"Yep." I shrugged. "That's what us monks like to do in our free time. Nothing better than a bit of praying. Good for the soul."

"Go and get him," the prince ordered.

I had to come up with something quickly. "I don't think that would be a good idea," I said. Now it was my turn to say a silent prayer. Please don't start howling down there.

"And why might that be?" he asked me, eyes never leaving mine.

"Well, he's praying for an end to this plague," I lied. "That's what your brother, the king, wants isn't it?"

He took a step towards me, stopping short of touching. "Very well," he said, drawing a deep breath. "It wasn't him I truly came to see."

"Who then?" I asked.

He looked down at me. "The king requests your attendance at the palace tomorrow evening."

"Really?" I exclaimed.

"The king has decided to take his court to Oxford, for the next week or so until the preacher has finally got a grip on this plague," the prince explained haughtily. "Therefore he is holding a party and would like you to attend."

"Why me?"

"Why do you think?" The prince reached out and fingered a stray length of my long hair.

I couldn't help but flinch at his touch. Smiling, he withdrew his hand, rubbing his fingers together as if ridding them of germs.

"I don't think the preacher would be happy . . ." I started; fearing the reason the king really wanted me to attend his party. That was never going to happen. I would actually rather have my head lopped off.

"He and the others are invited too. Rooms are being made up for you all," he said.

My options were running out and fast. "A party, you say?"

"That's right."

"Ah well, I don't really have any of my party gear with me, it's back in the village of Woolwich. This is all I've got," I said, picking at my cloak.

James threw the trunk he had been carrying down on the table and opened it. He reached inside and pulled out the most beautiful dress I had ever seen. It was blood red and looked to be made from a very fine silk. It shimmered in the pale sunlight streaming in through the window. The neck was cut low, but there were lacy white frills at the sleeves and all around its long flowing hem. It was tight at the waist and I could already imagine it swishing about my hips. I fought the urge to reach for it. The dress looked so soft that I wanted to hold it against my skin. I wanted to wear it – to look glamorous – not for the prince, the king or even Harry, but for me. I longed to rid myself of the dreary cloak and the dirt and the stench of decay from the graveyard, to look and feel gorgeous just for five minutes. To wear that dress would make me feel all of those things . . . but something told me that this dress came with far from innocent intentions.

"The king said you're to wear this."

"I bet he did," I whispered under my breath.

"What did you say?" the prince asked, cocking one eyebrow at me.

"I said I couldn't possibly accept a gift from the king." I suspected the dress wasn't the only thing the king wanted to give me.

"The king insists," he said, placing the dress back into the trunk as if it was a done deal and there was little point in any further discussion about it. At the door he turned to look at me. "I'd advise you not to disappoint him. He is looking forward to seeing you tomorrow night at eight. You can take the opportunity to return the carriage you have borrowed."

Then he was gone, striding away across the graveyard to his awaiting carriage. I flopped down into the nearest chair and, not for the first time since arriving in 1665, wished I was back in 2014. The thought of being with the king repulsed me more than the vampires that tried to kill me last night. If they came back tonight, I might just let them.

I sat in the chair until it grew dark outside and I could hear the distant cry of the watchman approaching in the distance.

"Bring out the dead! Bring out the dead!" he wailed.

24

I waited in the dark and swirling smoke for the watchman. And just like the night before I paid him for his help by giving him the last of the French francs I had found in my pocket. I opened the gate for him as he led the horse and cart full of the dead into the graveyard. Once at the fire he released the dead bodies into the flames. Their faces began to bubble, blister and blacken within moments as the greedy flames devoured them. Just like the night before, there were too many bodies to place on to the fire at once. With the spades we pushed them towards the fire so I could burn them later. It was then I saw the two bodies which looked as if they had been half eaten.

The watchman noticed. "I thought those two might grab your attention. Look just like the one I brought ya last night."

One of the two corpses was female, what was left of her hairless body told me that. But the other was just a baby. I had seen plenty of children piled up amongst the other bodies but this was different. This child hadn't died of any plague.

"I'm sorry, I need a minute," I muttered, turning and vomiting at the foot of the nearest tree.

The watchman hid behind his mask and said nothing.

I stood up shakily. "Where did you find them?" I asked him.

"Castle Street," he told me. I didn't know the location and had no map.

"Is it far?"

"Far enough," was his reply.

Even if I wanted to try and find it, I couldn't leave my post again tonight. Whether I liked the thought of it or not, I was going to have to stake those bodies; I couldn't just risk some of them coming back to life. But I could find out as much as possible from the watchman, although I doubted he would know very much.

"What kind of area is Castle Street in?" I inquired over the sound of the crackling and spitting fire.

"Very poor," he said.

Just like where the other nameless girl had been found.

"Which makes what happened even more surprising," he suddenly added.

"What do you mean?"

"Who would've thought the king would be interested

in a couple of wretches like these," he said, pointing down at the two half-eaten bodies.

"The king?" I said, staring at him. "What has the king to do with these deaths?"

"I'm not saying the king is involved, but someone close to him must have known these two," he said, backtracking from his original statement. I could hear the fear in his voice. Who wouldn't be scared of making such a wild accusation about the king of England?

"What do you mean then?"

"Well, some of the neighbours said they heard the young girl cry out. It was only the once so no one went to investigate. You got to understand there is a lot of screaming in London these days. Anyway, a short time later the baby started screaming, in pain like. So some of the neighbours got a bit twitchy at their curtains. They say that they saw a hooded fella come running from the house and jump straight into one of the king's carriages."

"What made them think it was one of the king's carriages?" I suspected I already knew the answer.

"Had the royal crest on the doors, didn't it," he said. "But I guess it doesn't mean nuffin'."

"Why not?"

"Probably just the king's physician taking a look. He's been known to check on the poor and the sick when the real quacks are busy. I guess the king is good to us like that – letting us use his personal doctor. Cares for his people like."

"I guess," I said thoughtfully. That was twice now that one of the king's carriages had been seen fleeing the scene of these hideous deaths. Where a body had been half eaten, there was the king's carriage waiting to take this hooded person away. That had to be more than just coincidence.

Before I'd had the chance to ask the watchman any more questions, the distinct sound of howling could be heard in the breeze. The watchman seemed to become agitated at once.

"I'll be going now," he said. "I've helped you – that was the arrangement."

"Are you all right?" I asked, knowing that he wasn't.

"The rumour is that giant hounds are killing those people," the watchman said, pointing down at the half eaten corpses at my feet.

"Who told you such a rumour?"

"Everyone is talking about it." He inched his way back across the graveyard. "The coffee houses are full of gossip."

"Perhaps gossip is all it is," I tried to assure him.

"Can't you hear it?" He wrung his filthy hands together.

"Hear what?" I shrugged my shoulders.

"Wolves." His voice sounded wheezy behind his mask.

"All I can hear is the sound of the wind," I said.

Without another word, the watchmen led the horse and cart out of the graveyard. I stood alone amongst the rotting burning dead and listened to my friends howling as if in agony from below.

25

I looked at the bodies scattered before the fire. Could I really bring myself to search each of them for the black tokens the preacher had spoken of? There was every chance that if they had them, they would rise up from the dead just like I had witnessed last night. I couldn't bring myself to search each of the decomposing bodies, but I would have to stake them and that would be bad enough.

The corpses of the half-eaten child and girl had been bitten by a vampire, I was sure of that, even though I couldn't see any black marks on what little flesh was remaining. I doubted very much either of them was going to come back and haunt me. And if they did, I couldn't bring myself to place the remains of the small child into the fire. I couldn't – I wouldn't. Kneeling, I scooped the baby up into my arms and carried it over to one of the graves the preacher had exhumed. With the wind blowing my hood about the sides of my face, and the full moon shining bright above me, I looked down into the hole. It was empty. Very carefully, I lowered the dead child into the ground. It looked so small, like a broken and cracked piece of marble in the dark. Reciting the Lord's Prayer in my mind, I shovelled earth into the hole and covered the child.

Once I had refilled the grave, I made my way back over to the dead who lay scattered on the ground amongst the broken headstones. I looked at the bleak scene and realised that my heart felt just as barren. It was like my senses had become numb – desensitised to the horrors I had seen since finding myself in 1665. Feeling like an empty husk, I went to the stable where Harry had filled a barrow with stakes. With the front wheel squeaking round and round, I pushed the barrow across the graveyard. Then, as if on autopilot, I knelt down and drove the first of those stakes into the heart of a corpse. I didn't even blink when the dead body suddenly twitched and cried out as I burst its black heart. And fearing that perhaps I had in some way become a heartless monster too, I drove one stake after another into the dead.

I worked through the night, the sounds of the wolves howling like a distant soundtrack playing in the background – nothing more now than white noise. Once I had staked the last of the dead, I propped myself against a leaning headstone and smoked. I blew tiny rings of smoke from my mouth and watched them drift up into the night, where they lost their shape and melted away. And I knew in my heart that if I wasn't careful, then I too would become like one of those smoke rings. I would gradually change; become something that I wasn't when I first arrived here – when I first met the preacher and the gang. It seemed to me that the longer I was in their company, the more I changed shape. I became someone – something – else. But however terrifying it could be in their company, it secretly thrilled me. Being with them could be a rush. They were the times I felt most alive. So did I feel dead and empty now not because of the soulless task I had just undertaken, but because they weren't with me? Was I missing being a part of the pack?

With the sky lightening, I shovelled the last of the corpses into the fire. Afterwards I looked down at my hands and to my revulsion they were smeared black with earth, ash and blood. So as the first thin strips of daylight broke across the sky and through the smoke, I filled a wooden pail at the public well across the street and I took it to the barn where I stripped naked and washed the filth and grime from my body. There was a chill wind in the air, but it was nowhere near as cold as the water I splashed through my hair and over my body. With my skin peppered with goose flesh, I grabbed my cloak and ran into the house. Once in my room, I dived beneath the blankets, pulling them tight about me. I was so tired I was asleep even before my body had stopped shivering.

I woke to silence. For the first time in what seemed like ages, I could hear nothing. It was then I realised my friends had fallen silent in the crypt below the church. I sat up in bed, my hair tangled about my shoulders and face. My throat felt dry, my lips cracked. Two nights had passed since I had locked my friends away. Did their silence mean that it was safe for me to release them? I hoped it was; I didn't want to be alone in 1665 anymore. I wanted to be with them. And however much I tried not to admit it – I wanted to see Harry. I got up, threw on the cloak and headed downstairs. The trunk with the dress the prince had brought as a gift from the king was still lying on the table where I had left it.

I had forgotten all about the party I had been invited to that night. The preacher and the others had to be ready to be released as I didn't like the idea of attending that party on my own. Two reasons. One, where was I to say the preacher and the gang were? I doubted the prince had believed my previous excuses as to their sudden disappearance. Two, I didn't like the idea of being at the party without my friends – *Harry* – being there to protect me from the king's advances. Now, back home in 2014, I would've told the pervert to go fuck himself, king or not. But in 2014 I wasn't going to end up in the Tower of London counting down the hours until I had my head chopped off. I'd probably get my picture in some lad's mag and end up in the Big Brother House.

I lit a candle and went through the door that led into

the passageway. I raced down it, the flame from the candle threatening to go out, I ran so fast. At the top of the stairs which led down into the crypt, I stopped. What if my friends were still wolves? What if they weren't ready to be released? Would they tell me they were even if they weren't?

Taking a deep breath, I slowly made my way down into the crypt.

26

With the candle only penetrating the darkness just inches ahead of me, I called out over the sound of my pounding heart.

"Hello?"

A sound of movement, like someone shifting. I stepped forward towards the bars that I knew were somewhere ahead of me. The flame wavered.

The noise came again.

"Preacher?" I called.

Drip! Drip! The sound of running water so loud now in the silence it was like a drum beat.

Slowly, carefully, I placed one foot in front of the other.

"Harry?" I breathed.

A hand shot out towards me, looking like a bunch of bony twigs in the candlelight.

"You sound as if you need one of these," I heard the preacher say.

In the gloom I could see a cigarette dangling between his thumb and forefinger. My own fingers were trembling as I took it. If the preacher was trying to trick me somehow wouldn't he have grabbed hold of me as I took the cigarette from his hand? I saw a red light wink on and off in the darkness. The preacher was smoking. Then like some ghostly apparition his face swam out of the darkness. It glowed a sickly yellow in the light from my candle. I looked into his hard blue eyes, which sparkled like they always did. They were not flaming bright and angry like they were when he had turned.

"Is it safe to let you out?" I asked, still not sure whether to trust him or not. He had told me – screamed at me – not to release him, whatever he said.

"I want to see Harry."

There was more movement in the darkness. I swept the candle towards it. Harry loomed up behind the bars, his face rugged, hair dishevelled as always. I looked into his grey eyes and he matched my gaze.

"Do you love me?" I whispered.

"Don't be so fucking stupid," he grunted, sliding his hand through the bars and waiting for the key.

It wasn't the answer I secretly hoped for, but it was the one I knew the true Harry would give. If he were still the wolf he would have told me exactly what I wanted to hear. Without breaking his stare once, I placed the key in the palm of his hand. I heard the key slide into the lock, then the cell door swinging slowly open. In the candlelight, I saw him come towards me.

"What's for dinner? I'm starving." He brushed past me and climbed up the stairs out of the crypt.

He was definitely his old self again. "What's for dinner?" I cried in disbelief, stomping after him. I could hear the others following behind.

"Well it's not as if you haven't had plenty of time to prepare something," he said, reaching the top of the staircase. "What have you been doing over the last couple of days?"

"I haven't been sitting on my arse thinking about your cock or anyone else's for that matter!" I roared at him.

"Glad to hear it," he said, striding away down the passageway.

"Why you arrogant, self-centred prick!" I said, chasing after him.

"So what *have* you been doing?" he said, marching into the living room and noticing that there was nothing cooking over the fire.

"Look, I'm not your slave!" I barked prodding him in the chest with my finger. "I've spent the last couple of days burning dead people, being ripped off by the watchman, lighting fires, burying kids, being chased by vampires, listening to you howl your guts out. And do I get as much as a thank you? No! All I get is more of your bullshit!"

"What do you mean, you were chased by vampires?" the preacher said, coming into the room. Louise and Zoe were at his heels.

"Hey Sammy." Zoe waved her hand. At least someone seemed pleased to see me. I waved back, forcing a smile. I had no fight with her.

"Tea, anyone?" Louise said.

"What the fuck is this?" I stammered. "You've just spent the last couple of days locked up like caged animals, I've just lived through a freaking nightmare and you lot are acting as if nothing has happened."

"What vampires chased you?" the preacher asked again.

I dropped into one of the chairs by the fire. "The ones that the watchman brought here."

"They were still alive?" Harry asked, glancing at the preacher then back at me.

"They were by the time I got back," I said.

"Back from where?" Louise asked.

This was beginning to feel like an interrogation.

"I went to check out a house—" I started.

"What house?" Even Zoe had joined in now.

Swallowing hard, I looked at my friends gathered around me and told them everything that had happened over the last few days. I explained about the dead young woman who had been eaten, what I'd discovered at the house and what her neighbour had told me about the king's carriage. I went on to tell them about how when I returned some of the vampires had come back to life. I admitted that was my fault as I hadn't staked them. The preacher looked daggers at me and tutted as if I were some errant child. I continued. While I sat and told them about the half-eaten girl and baby, I couldn't help but notice the preacher and Harry glance at each other. I told them that a carriage and a hooded figure had been seen fleeing the house and that the watchman thought perhaps it was the king's surgeon who had been seen and there was nothing suspicious about what had happened. When I had finished, I pointed over at the trunk on the table and said, "And before I forget, we've all been invited to a party tonight."

Zoe suddenly beamed with excitement. "Whose party?"

"The king's."

"Why is the king throwing a party?" Louise asked.

"So he can try and get into my knickers," I sighed.

"What makes you say that?" Harry said, eyeing me.

I looked at him. Was he jealous? Who was I kidding?

"His brother brought me the dress that's in the box," I explained. "He says the king insists that I wear it."

"What's so bad about that?" Zoe asked.

"It's cut so freaking low that everyone will not only be staring at my tits but my navel too."

"So the prince has been here?" The preacher looked rattled by this.

"If you're worried about the state of that carriage, he didn't see it," I said. "Although he does want it taken back tonight."

"It's not the carriage I'm worried about," the preacher said.

"What then?" I asked.

He looked at me as if deep in thought. "Did he ask where we were?"

I nodded. "I said you were praying."

"What, for two freaking days?" Harry grunted.

"He wasn't here for the whole two days," I said.

"Sure about that?" Harry fingered the dress in the box, then looked up at me.

He was jealous. I was sure of it. Harry had been jealous of how the king had flirted with me at the palace. And he was jealous now, thinking that I might have spent the last couple of days in the prince's company while he was locked up in the crypt. Still mad at him, I got up, snatched the dress from the box and said, "At least someone round here knows how to make a woman feel good about herself."

Harry looked away, as if he wasn't bothered by my remark, but I knew he was. Louise caught my eye and winked at me. She knew what I was up to.

"I think we have more to worry about than a dress," the preacher said, trying to melt the sudden frostiness in the room.

"You think the king might be involved in the deaths of these young girls?" I'd had the same thoughts.

"No, I don't think the king is involved," he said with a shake of his head.

"Someone close to him then?" I pushed, eager to have the preacher agree with me.

"No, I don't think any of the royal court is involved." He

lit another smoke and went to the window, where he stood and looked out at the darkening sky. "They're not vampires."

"But the carriages?" I gasped, looking at the others for them to agree with me.

"The watchman is right, the carriage that the people thought they saw was probably just the king's surgeon."

"What? He makes house calls does he?" I sneered in disbelief at what I was hearing. I thought my friends would be as suspicious as I was. I thought I had done well while they were locked away, that perhaps I had come some way in unmasking the vampire they sought.

"It might not have even been one of the king's carriages," Louise said, as if trying to let me down gently.

"But witnesses said they saw the king's crest on the doors," I reminded them.

"I'm surprised anyone saw anything, what with it being night and all the smoke from the fires . . ." Zoe said.

"You don't believe me do you?" I felt hurt and let down after everything I had been through over the last two days and nights while they had been languishing below.

The preacher turned away from the window. "It's not that we don't believe you, Sammy, it's just that someone could have been mistaken in what they saw. They then mention it to someone else who then passes the story on. If such rumours get back to the king, he will have their heads for sure. You can't go around accusing the king of being responsible for eating people. You can't go around believing that he is a vampire."

"I can believe what I want," I shot back, looking at all of them. Then I added, "You act as if you're scared of the king and his brother."

"He is the king, not a vampire," Harry said.

"But what if someone in his court is?" I said.

"Then perhaps they will reveal themselves to us tonight," the preacher said. "Now go and put your new dress on."

I went to the bottom of the stairs. Before climbing them, I paused. "Perhaps you're right to be afraid of the king."

"Why do you say that?" The preacher half smiled.

"The watchman said that rumours are rife in the coffee houses and on the streets that a giant pack of hounds – wolves – is eating the dead. You yourself told the king that wild dogs were digging up the dead. What if a rumour starts that it was a wolf in the carriage seen leaving the houses of those dead people? What if someone was to discover there was an identical carriage hidden behind this church? What if the gossip mongers put two and two together and came up with four wolves?" I looked at the four of them. "What if you were given that carriage for a reason? What if you've all been set up?"

I climbed the stairs to my room, where I slammed the door closed behind me.

27

I put on the dress James had brought to the house for me. It was made of the finest crimson red silk and felt soft against my skin. It was indeed cut very low over my chest. The way my breasts almost bulged out of it didn't leave very much to the imagination but I had to admit that the overall effect was better than I'd thought it would be. I let my long blond hair hang loose about my shoulders; there was very little I could do with it. For the first time since arriving in 1665, I felt pretty, but would anyone other than the king notice? Though I wasn't one for wearing fancy dresses back home, here I felt different. The dress might come with strings, but just for one night why couldn't I be a princess if I wanted to? Wasn't that every little girl's fantasy? It had certainly been one of mine as I sat as a little girl brushing my hair before the mirror, my mother's jewellery box open in my lap. There was a soft tapping at my door and those memories floated away like faint whispers on a breeze.

"Can I come in?" It was Zoe.

"Sure," I said.

Zoe poked her head around the edge of the door and looked at me. "Wow, Sammy, you look so pretty in that dress."

"You look pretty too," I told her. As she entered my room, I could see that she was wearing a long blue dress. It was sleeveless and had lace ruffles at the neckline.

"I thought you might want some of these," she said, holding out her hand where several hairpins lay in her palm.

"You must be a mind reader," I said.

"Would you like me to do your hair for you?" she asked, sounding excited.

"Why not?" I sat down at the end of my bed and soon felt Zoe's slender fingers curling and pinning my hair up.

"I love going to parties," she said, fixing my hair. "I haven't been to a really good party since the end of that war."

"What war was that?" I asked.

"The Second World War, you were there, remember, and Harry went and—" She stopped mid-sentence as if realising her mistake. "You don't remember do you?"

I shook my head. "No."

Zoe slid her fingers from my hair and I heard her cross the room to the door.

"Zoe," I called after her.

"I shouldn't have said anything."

"It's not that. I know you can't tell me about my past – future – whatever it may be, and one day I hope I will remember everything. But I just wanted to ask . . ."

"What?" She looked through the gap in the door as if to make sure our conversation couldn't be overheard.

"Why doesn't the preacher believe me?" I asked. "Why doesn't he believe the vampire we're searching for might be connected to the king in some way?"

"Sammy, how can you expect anyone else to believe you if you don't even believe in yourself?" Zoe said, suddenly sounding much older than her sixteen years.

"I do!" I tried to assure her.

"If you truly did, Sammy, you wouldn't have forgotten that party after the war. You forget because you don't believe. You don't believe because you want to forget."

"What is it I don't want to remember?"

"The truth," she said, before leaving me alone in my room.

I came downstairs, the long red dress trailing behind me. It made a rustling noise as I crossed the room. Harry was waiting for me by the door. Beyond him I could see that the others were already waiting in the carriage. It looked kind of ridiculous, as both doors were missing. In fact one whole side of the carriage was nothing more than rough splinters. The roof was torn open where Harry had burst through it. The only things left intact were the wheels and the seat up top where the preacher was perched. As I crossed the room towards him I sensed that Harry hadn't taken his eyes off me since appearing before him in my new dress. I was expecting him to make some sarcastic remark when he took me by the wrist, preventing me from leaving the house.

"What?" I said, looking into his eyes.

"You look beautiful, Samantha," he said, the gruffness gone from his voice.

"Really?" I felt shocked but secretly elated by his comment.

"Really." He let go of my wrist and went outside to climb into the carriage.

With my heart racing ever so slightly, I followed him. I didn't fancy riding inside as the whole thing was one big death trap and what with the luck I'd been having lately, I feared I might just fall out of the side and beneath the carriage wheels.

With the dress swishing around my feet, I made my way to the front of the carriage, where the preacher sat wrapped in his black cloak. He offered me his outstretched hand and pulled me up.

"Thank you," I said, taking my seat beside him.

The preacher rattled the reins and the horse drew the dilapidated carriage out through the graveyard gates and on to the road. It was full dark now, and just like the night I had gone to investigate that house, the streets swirled with a dense choking smoke. As we made our way across the desolate city and towards Whitehall Palace, I glanced sideways at the preacher.

"I'm sorry you don't believe me," I said, not looking for another quarrel. I was genuinely sorry.

"I'm sorry too," he said back, passing me a smoke.

He turned and squinted at me through the smoke coiling up from the end of his cigarette.

"What?" I asked feeling a little uncomfortable.

"There are some things that perhaps I should have told you," he said with a hint of regret.

"Like what?" I asked.

"Just things." As we approached St James's Park I could see the palace in the distance, those white turrets looking pristine against the dirty smog that swathed the city.

"You can't just say *things*, and then nothing more," I said. "It's not fair."

"Now isn't the time," he said, yanking on the reins and making a clucking sound deep in his throat.

"When, then?" I needed to know. Would it be the answer to all of this?

"When we've finished here in 1665." He glanced sideways from beneath his hood at me.

"When will that be?" I pushed.

"When we've done what we came to do," he said, eyes sharp.

"If you believe me, we might catch the vampire sooner than you think," I said, hoping that I might get him to change his mind about what I had earlier told him.

As if he hadn't heard me, the preacher faced front again, the horse pulling the carriage beneath the big white archway that led into the palace courtyard.

"Me, Louise and Zoe are going to sneak away from the party later," he said.

"Why?" I asked.

"You've seen what happens if the dead aren't destroyed properly," he said. "The watchman won't stop bringing the dead because the king has decided to throw himself a party."

"What about Harry?"

"He will stay with you just in case the king's hands decide to wander too far." He drew the carriage and the horse to a stop.

"Thank you." I was glad the preacher had asked Harry to stay back with me.

The same stableman who had given the carriage to us now stood in the courtyard, mouth open as he scratched his head in dismay at the sight of it.

"What . . . what?" he started to mumble as he surveyed the damage, lost somewhere between disbelief and shock.

We climbed down and the others almost fell out of the gaping hole that was now the side of the king's carriage.

"What happened?" the stableman spluttered.

"You might well ask," the preacher barked at him. "You could've got us killed."

"Me?" the lad asked in wonder.

"It's your job to maintain these things isn't it?" The preacher pointed back at the wrecked carriage.

"Well, yes, but—" the stableman started.

"We hadn't even gone a couple of miles when it started to fall to pieces." Anger was building in the preacher's voice. "If it hadn't have been for my excellent handling of the horse we could've all been dead thanks to you."

"But . . ."

"If I were you," the preacher said, leaning into the lad's face, "I'd go and patch the carriage up quick, before the king sees it."

"Patch it up! It's been practically destroyed."

"Don't worry." The preacher patted the boy on the shoulder. "I won't tell the king what you did."

The preacher strode away. We followed, leaving the lad scratching his head as he stood staring wide-eyed at what was left of the carriage.

28

A man wearing more frills than a bride on her wedding day led us into a vast banqueting hall. The walls and giant pillars stretched high above us to reveal the most glorious ceiling I had ever seen. Staring up at if from below was like looking up into heaven. It had been painted a light blue with masses of clouds. Amongst them, plump little cherubs had been painted. Each of them was rosy-cheeked and held a harp in their podgy hands. They almost seemed to float amongst the heavens with the aid of perfect white-feathered wings.

With my mouth still open, I looked across the banqueting hall. The longest table I had ever seen stretched away into the distance. It was covered in enough food to feed two armies. There were chops, steaks, fish, lobsters, fruit, cake, wine, beer and anything else you could care to imagine.

It seemed surreal to think that the people of London were dying outside of these palace walls. The streets I had ridden, the people I had seen and the squalor they had to endure were worlds away from this.

We passed along the table, Harry at my side. Should I take his arm? Perhaps I should wait for him to take mine? But if I stuck close to Harry, acted as if we were together, then perhaps the king would keep his distance and leave me alone. Leave me and Harry to spend the night together. My head began to spin with the idea of us dancing together, my new beautiful dress flowing out behind me as Harry held me tight in his arms.

I turned to slide my arm through Harry's but realised I had been too slow. Lady Castlemaine had taken him by the arm and was leading him on to the dance floor. She hadn't wasted any time getting her claws into him. Harry still wore his cloak, but it was unfastened down the front. He wore a white shirt which was open at the throat and breeches just like the other men. No shoes with buckles for him, instead a pair of dark-brown leather boots which stopped just below the knee. I watched, heart racing, as Lady Castlemaine wrapped her arms about Harry's neck as if hanging from him. She simpered up into his face, eyelids fluttering. Harry glanced over at me and I looked away as if I didn't care. When I sneaked a look back in his direction just moments later, he had his arms around her waist and they were dancing. My heart jumped into my throat.

"Here, have some of this," I heard someone say as a glass of wine was shoved into my hands.

I found Louise standing next to me. She looked really beautiful tonight, her long dark hair bouncing about her creamy shoulders, a dark-blue dress hugging her hips.

"Don't let him upset you," she said, with a knowing smile.

"Who?" I tried to pretend I had no idea who she was talking about.

"You know who," she said. "This is none of my business, but Harry really does care about you."

"Really looks like it," I said, unable to take my eyes off Lady Castlemaine's wandering hands as they rested on Harry's tight arse. He did nothing to push her hands away. Instead he ran his hands up the back of her lilac dress. She almost seemed to writhe against him. He looked over at me, then back down at her. Throwing my head back I took a large gulp of wine.

"It's not what it seems, Sammy," Louise said. "It hasn't been easy for Harry . . ."

"I'm not interested." I shrugged, taking another gulp of wine. It was stronger than any wine I'd tasted before. Good. I needed it. I drained my glass and took another from the table.

"If it makes it any easier, I'm not going to get my man either tonight." She meant the preacher, who had moved away from us, slinking into a corner of the vast banqueting hall where he stood and watched proceedings from a distance. "I fear we have a long night ahead of us, and not one moment of it will involve us fucking," she sighed.

I thought of Louise and the preacher naked beneath the stars then pushed the image away, a flash of guilt pricking my heart. I looked again at Lady Castlemaine as she stood fondling Harry on the dance floor, then back at Louise.

"The preacher might be your man, Louise, but Harry isn't mine," I said before draining my second glass of wine. I snatched up another and skulked away, leaving Louise alone by the table loaded with food.

I made my way around the edge of the dance floor. The vast walls were painted from floor to ceiling with pictures of naked women. They were just as plump as the cherubs above. It looked like Rubens had been let loose in the room under strict orders to let his mind run wild. There was a small band of musicians and minstrels. They played violins, flutes and even bagpipes. The music was light and cheerful. I was probably listening to an original classical masterpiece, but I had no idea what. I wasn't really up on the whole classical music thing. The Smiths and Arctic Monkeys were more me. I wondered if the band took requests and smiled to myself. As I wandered about, I saw Zoe dancing with a young man. I had never seen him before. He looked hot and she looked happy. It would be nice if Zoe found someone for herself – if she found love. Castlemaine was groping Harry's arse again. Actually, perhaps it would be best if Zoe stayed single. She didn't need a broken heart – she had enough shit to deal with being a Skinturner. Have some fun – love could wait. I continued my way round the dance floor, when I saw the saddest thing – the queen standing by herself against the far wall of the banqueting hall. The misery in her eyes was unmistakable. I had seen it before as a teenager, the girl at the party who just didn't seem to fit in – left on her own with a pile of handbags while her friends partied on hard. But the woman I spied across the hall was the queen – this was her party. So what if she dressed differently from the other women in her trousers and shirt and buckled shoes. She came from a foreign country and culture. The life she had before coming to England from Portugal had probably been vastly different to the one she now led. Watching her standing all alone, I guessed that not so much had changed over the last three hundred and fifty years. Some strangers to these shores were still made to feel uncomfortable and not allowed to fit in.

I wanted to go to her. But what did I have in common with a woman who lived nearly three hundred and fifty years in my past? It wasn't like I could bowl up to her and start chatting about Daniel-freaking-Craig. Still, we were both women, right? So surely we would find something. Draining the last of the wine from my glass to give myself some confidence, I started off across the dance floor. I hadn't gone very far when I felt something cover my eyes. I had been blindfolded.

"Hey!" I gasped. "What's going on?"

I could hear laughter.

"It's a game," someone said close by. "Play along. Have some fun."

Then I was being spun around as if by many hands. The music sped up a little, and I felt suddenly dizzy. The wine I'd drunk seemed to be sloshing around in my brain. I staggered a little but felt hands on me pushing me upright again. Around and around I was spun. At last I reached for the blindfold and, clawing at it, managed to pull it down over my face. I found myself being pushed into the king's welcoming arms.

He wasted no time in wrapping them around me and pulling me close. I felt my breasts press up against him. At the sight of those swelling mounds of flesh, a look of delight crossed his face. He licked his lips furtively, and I could only begin to imagine what thoughts were racing through his mind.

"I can't breathe, Majesty," I said, trying to ease myself off him.

"Let us dance," he said, springing away across the dance floor with me in his arms. My head spun as he swirled me around. It was like my feet were no longer touching the polished floor. The music continued to play as others danced all about us. I saw Harry, still in the arms of Lady Castlemaine. He glanced over at me, his eyes dark and stormy. As the king twirled me, I desperately scanned the smiling faces for the preacher, Louise and Zoe. I couldn't see them anywhere amongst the other party goers. Had they sneaked away already, back to the church and the graveyard to make sure the dead were really dead?

The king pulled me closer still as we danced. His cheek brushed against mine and his skin was cold and a little clammy. Was he excited? I feared so. As he pulled me by the waist against him, there was now something hard digging into my belly. Cheek to cheek, I could feel his breath against me.

When Harry saw the king pressed against me he tried to break free of Lady Castlemaine's grip, but she pulled him back before he had taken even two steps towards me.

"I've decided that I shall take you to my bed tonight," the king whispered, like I had won some kind of prize.

Didn't I have a say in any of this? I wondered. I bit my tongue, and scoured my mind for some kind of excuse, anything that would get me out of this, but also prevent me from ending the night by being thrown into the Tower.

"I'm flattered your Majesty, but I'm afraid I'm with another tonight." I felt the tip of his tongue trail over my cheek and I shuddered.

"Who might that be?" He slid his hands down the length of my back and squeezed my arse.

"Harry Turner," I said, hoping that he would come and rescue me. That had been the instruction the preacher had given him.

I felt the king tilt his head to one side. "Harry looks like he's going to be too preoccupied tonight to worry about what we might get up to," he said. Then as if to prove his point, he spun me around. Across the dance floor I could see Lady Castlemaine groping Harry again as she smiled up at him. But Harry wasn't looking down at her, he was looking at me. Our eyes met, then Lady Castlemaine was dragging him away once more. I saw another face and it almost broke my heart. The queen was watching me and the king as we swayed cheek to cheek. And I knew exactly how she felt.

"I need some air," I told the king, trying to pull free of him again. I just couldn't bear the sight of the unhappiness in the queen's eyes.

"Of course." He smiled, looping his arm through mine and guiding me off the dance floor towards two giant bay windows. He had no shame. It was clear he couldn't give a shit about his wife and her feelings.

He pushed the windows open and we stepped outside on to a vast lush lawn. In the light thrown from the chandeliers inside the hall, I could see a huge fountain. Water bubbled and splashed from it. I'd hardly caught my breath before the king had his hands all over me again. I tried to pull away, but he held me tight. He brought his face towards me, lips pursed, tongue showing. I turned my head to the side in disgust. This was unbearable. I really didn't care if I was thrown into the Tower to rot for eternity. I wasn't going to let this man maul me – king or not.

"Get off me," I warned, pushing him away. But his grip on me didn't loosen.

He came towards me again.

There was the sound of a cough, so soft and subtle it was hardly audible over the sound of the fountain and my beating heart. But the king heard it and he turned back towards the bay windows where the queen was standing just feet away. I slipped from the king's clutches and hung my head in shame. It felt degrading to be found in the arms of another woman's husband. Even though I hadn't done anything wrong, I couldn't help but also feel responsible in some way.

"I think the young lady has had enough dancing for one evening, do you not agree, Charles?" the queen said. "She looks quite exhausted."

"Perhaps?" the king said, his eyes falling once again to my breasts. "Are you all spent?"

"Quite so, Majesty," I said, lowering my gaze so as not to meet his piercing stare.

"Very well," the king said with a shrug of his shoulders, as if it mattered not to him. Then he kissed me gently on the cheek and in doing so he whispered in my ear, "Do not keep me waiting, I am not a patient man."

A cold set of fingers curled around mine and I saw the queen was now beside me and holding my hand. "I think the young lady would like to go back into the warm." She smiled sweetly at the king, then led me away, holding my hand tight.

"Don't be afraid," she reassured me. "You have done nothing wrong. Let me escort you to your room. I promise you will be quite safe from my husband there."

29

The queen showed me to my room, my head feeling light and giddy. She still held my hand in hers, and her skin felt so smooth, like marble. I was grateful for her understanding. I still felt embarrassed about the compromising situation she had caught me in with the king. People had doubtless lost their heads for less. Even though I felt more than just giddy, I suspected she understood exactly what her husband was like around women. After all, the preacher had told me the queen, as well as many others, was aware of the relationship between him and Lady Castlemaine.

As we stopped outside my bedroom door, I looked upon her face. Again, I couldn't help but feel she was different from the other women in the king's court. There was definitely a sadness about her. And who could really blame her? She had come from another country to marry a man who openly flirted with other women and took them to his bed. I didn't know how she lived like that. In silence, I guessed. Perhaps that's why she was so meek and withdrawn? Maybe she felt too afraid to speak out to defend herself.

I pictured Harry dancing with Lady Castlemaine. I couldn't rid my mind of the image. Whore. But had Harry enjoyed dancing with her? Was he like the king? Were there other women in his life when I wasn't around? If he travelled back to another time like I did, was there a woman waiting for him there? Was I Harry's Lady Castlemaine? I couldn't be sure if it was because of the sadness I felt for the queen or my own anger at Harry that tears suddenly stung my eyes. Perhaps it had been the wine? One tear must have spilt on to my cheek, as the queen reached out with her free hand and gently wiped it away.

"Do not cry, it does not help heal the soul," she said quietly. "I should know."

Then, letting my fingers slip from her hand, she turned away. From behind, and dressed in the trousers and shirt, she could easily have been mistaken for a young man. Perhaps there was another reason the king preferred the company of Lady Castlemaine to that of his wife?

"Good night," I replied. Once she had gone, I entered the room she had led me to.

Candles had been lit for me. The room was as wide as

it was long. There was a four-poster bed and a fireplace set into the wall with a small pile of logs slowly burning in the grate, ridding the room of any winter chill. The flickering flames cast long shadows of orange and red across the walls. What looked like thick velvet drapes hung from the wooden posts at each corner of the bed. I crossed the room to the large bay window and looked out across the courtyard. On the other side of it were the stables. The young stableman who had given us the carriage was standing outside, his face a white moon in the dark. As if sensing he was being watched, he looked up at the window where I stood and a slow grin crept across his face. Those rotting teeth I had noticed a few nights before were now gleaming white. With a soft gasp in the back of my throat, I retreated and collided with someone. A blindfold fell over my eyes and was securely fastened. With a fist raised, I turned around. A hand gripped hold of my wrist, then the other. Whoever it was pulled me close. Had the king followed me to my room? Had he waited for the queen to retire to her bedroom for the night before slinking into mine?

I could feel their breath hot against my face. "Who are you?" I demanded.

The only reply I got was the sound of rapid breathing. Then, as if my survival instincts had taken control, I raised one knee and crushed it into the groin of whoever had hold of me. The hands immediately released their grip on my wrists, and I heard an agonising groan. With my hands free I yanked off the blindfold, to discover Harry doubled up before me, both hands between his legs.

"What was that for?" he moaned.

"I should have done that down in the banqueting hall!" I snapped at him. "Now get out!"

"Now listen here . . ." he started.

"I'm not interested in anything you've got to say. I saw the way you were dancing with the Castlemaine woman. I saw the way she had her hands all over you."

"You're exaggerating," he groaned, trying to straighten up.

"Really? From where I was standing it looked like she was giving you a freaking rectal examination!"

"I get it." He looked at me, his eyes watery and blood-shot in the firelight. "You're jealous."

I scoffed, throwing my hands to my hips. "Jealous! What? Have you suddenly developed a sense of humour? Because if you have, you're not making me laugh!"

"You just couldn't bear to see me in the arms of another woman." He managed a half smirk around the pain I'd caused him.

"Don't flatter yourself, numb-nuts." Secretly I was as jealous as hell, and hated myself for being so.

"Go on, admit it," he dared, standing straight and coming towards me. "Admit that you're jealous."

"Never!" I spat, turning my back to him, not wanting him to see the jealousy.

I could feel his breath on my bare shoulders. I shrank

away from him. He took another step closer. Then I noticed a full-length mirror fixed to the wall. I could see my reflection and Harry looking like nothing more than my own shadow standing behind me.

"I hated seeing you in the king's arms," he suddenly confessed.

To hear him say such a thing almost took my breath away. Did he mean what he had just said? I must have misheard him.

He spoke again. "It made me jealous. So jealous that I had to do everything in my power to not leap across the dance floor and rip out his fucking heart for laying his hands on you."

My heart raced in my chest. Was he trying to talk me into bed with him again? To be honest, Harry had never had to do much talking to do that. But I wasn't going to give in so easily tonight. I was angry and hurting.

"If you mean what you say, why do you act like such an arrogant jerk the whole time? Why are you so impossible?"

"It's not easy having a relationship with someone who is always coming and going," he said, stepping out of the shadows so I could now clearly see his reflection. "You never stay around long enough, Sammy, for me – for us – to really get to know each other. You say I'm impossible, but you're impossible to love."

"Love?" I breathed.

"If only you stayed long enough for us to find out," he said.

Turning slowly to face him, I looked into his eyes. "What happened in Paris?"

"This," he whispered, crushing his lips over mine. Harry eased his tongue into my mouth. He pushed it against mine and I pushed back. His unkempt chin brushed up against my cheek. It felt rough, manly. Harry held me by the back of my neck, pulling my face forward as he pushed his tongue deeper into my mouth. It was like he was hungry for me. I placed my hands against his chest, not to push him away, but to feel his heartbeat. Only then would I know if his feelings were true. A tongue could tell a lie, but a heart only spoke a truth. His chest was as hard as rock but, beneath it, I could feel the power of his pounding heart. With my own matching the same strong beat, I let my fingers roam across his taut stomach. I no longer wanted this to be a fantasy. I wanted it to be real. It was then I understood the answer Zoe had given to the question I'd asked her. This could all be real if I really wanted it to be. Perhaps I wouldn't keep forgetting, shifting, if only I believed. The preacher had told me not to believe with my eyes, but with faith.

So, closing my eyes tight, I told myself to believe in this world I now found myself in, but most of all to believe in Harry. As if suddenly floating up into the air, I felt my feet lift off the floor as Harry swept me up into his arms. He carried me away from the mirror and laid me gently down on the bed. I pulled off the dress the king had given me, the petticoat and knickers until I was lying naked on the bed. I lay and watched Harry pull off his clothes. When he was stripped bare, he laced his fingers with mine and pulled me towards him. He sat on the edge of the bed and gently guided me down on to his lap. I felt him in me. With his arms folded around me in an embrace, we sat facing the full-length mirror positioned at the end of the bed. With his arms wrapped gently about my shoulders, Harry slid his knees between my thighs, easing my legs apart. Very gently he lifted me off his lap, then slowly down again. I looked into the mirror and could see him sliding slowly in and out of me. Harry ran one hand over my breasts, down the length of my body, coming to rest it between my legs. He began to gently stroke me. I enjoyed watching him touch me. I moved my hips slowly up and down, taking control of how slow and hard he moved deep within me.

"Do you like watching?" Harry asked, looking over my shoulder at my reflection.

"Yes." I shuddered, his fingers brushing over me, as I continued to move up and down on his lap. I pushed myself down, taking all of him, an almost immediate need to burst with pleasure rushing over me. But I didn't want it to be over for either of us just yet. I wanted more.

As if sensing this, Harry eased me from his lap, sliding his hand from deep within my thighs, and laying me on the bed. Kneeling over me, Harry took my hands in his, brought them up to his lips, and kissed them. With his eyes closed, he kissed each hand, wrist, and arm. Unlike how he had kissed me before, each of his kisses was slow, deliberate, making my skin tingle as if being brushed over with a feather. There was no rushing from Harry now. He seemed to be savouring every moment – savouring me. There was no desperate fucking. It was like he was trying to show me how much I did actually mean to him. For the first time ever with Harry what was now happening between us – what we were sharing – felt like more than just sex. Tilting my head back, I let my eyes slowly close as I relished every brush of his lips. No one had ever covered me from head to toe in kisses before. It felt wonderful, like I was something delicate – something fragile and precious. I didn't want these feelings to end. I never wanted to travel – *shift* – back to where I had come from. I wanted to stay with Harry.

His tongue worked its way back up my legs, over my thighs, coming to linger over the tiny patch of blond hair there. My flesh tingled and stomach muscles tightened. I slowly eased my legs apart. Not much, just enough. Within moments, I felt the tip of Harry's tongue roll gently down between my legs. Arching my back, I sighed and opened my legs an inch or two more. I felt the tip of his tongue enter me. Harry moved slowly. Just like he had kissed me, it was like he wanted to savour, taste every moment. Did he fear that I suddenly could go again? Shift back to 2014, perhaps never to come back? Neither of us wanted what was now happening between us to end. I entwined my fingers in his unruly hair and felt his tongue slip from within me. I half opened my eyes and looked down the length of my body. Harry raised his head from between my thighs, and looked at me.

"Come here," I whispered.

As he moved up and over me, I felt his cock slowly slide into me. This was the first time I could remember him being inside me while I looked up into his face. It was much more intimate. I murmured as he slowly drew deep into me. Harry groaned softly. I locked my legs around his back, wanting all of him. He stared down into my face. "I want to stay locked inside you forever, Samantha."

"Why?" I asked.

"Because if we're locked together then you can't go," he said.

"Hold me. Don't ever let go and I won't be able to go back." I wrapped my arms around him and held him tight to me. As we lay joined together, it was like we clung to each other, too scared now to ever let go.

"I won't let you go again." Harry began to move himself in and out of me. I dug my fingers into his back, as if trying to pull all of him into me. To make us truly one.

I covered his face, neck and shoulders with kisses. "Harder," I said, that feeling of urgency building deep inside of me again.

"You're more beautiful than anything, Sammy," he murmured.

That beating thud between my legs began to burn,

sending out a flurry of feverish tremors to my very centre. I clung to him. "Harder! Don't stop!" I pleaded with him.

Harry thrust deeper into me, our arms and legs entwined, our bodies burning up. I wanted to feel those feverish tremors in my stomach, in my heart, in my throat. I wanted to be consumed by those feelings – by him. It felt as if it was only me and Harry alive. No one else existed and nothing else mattered apart from that raging passion about to collapse inside of me. My heart raced so fast I feared it might burst. Harry drove himself deeper and faster into me as I raked his back, gripped him between my thighs, and kissed his lips. That frantic fever churning in my stomach unravelled outwards, making every one of my nerve endings seethe with life. I suddenly rocked and bucked beneath Harry as my body quivered uncontrollably. At the very same moment, Harry's entire body seemed to spasm in my arms as he gasped. Both of us cried out as we came together in each other's arms.

Harry rolled off me. We both lay breathless, still locked in each other's arms, both of us unwilling to let go of the other just yet. Harry looked into my eyes and I looked back into his. Both of our bodies shone with sweat in the candle and firelight. I could hear my heart hammering in my ears as I panted for breath. And however intense and real our lovemaking had just been, part of me feared that Harry would slide from my arms and leave me. That's what he had done before.

"Why such a sad face?" he asked me, combing a stray strand of hair from my cheek and behind my ear.

"I'm waiting for you to get up and leave me, just like you have before," I said.

"I could say the same of you."

Then as if both reading each other's minds or sensing exactly what each other needed at that precise moment in time, we gripped each other's hands tight, locking our fingers together.

"I'm not going anywhere," he said, eyes sliding closed.

"Me neither." I smiled, leaning in and kissing him gently on the mouth. He was already asleep, before my lips had left his.

Curled on my side, I lay and watched him sleep. I wondered from what time in history he came. I wondered whether he had always been a Skinturner or had been bitten by another like the preacher had bitten Zoe and, in turn, Zoe had bitten Louise. Maybe if Harry bit me . . . ? I pushed that thought from my head and sat up.

But perhaps if I became one of them I could stay?

No!

I let go of Harry's hand and got up, pulled my petticoat from off the floor and put it on. I lit a cigarette, blowing smoke into the air while trying to push those crazy thoughts from my head. In the distance I heard the sound of a church bell toll three times. With a stream of blue smoke drifting from my cigarette, I crossed to the window and looked out across the courtyard. There was no moon tonight so everything was covered by a blanket of virtual darkness. From the direction of the stable, I thought I saw movement.

The stableman again? I wondered.

Careful not to be seen by him this time, I stood at the edge of the window frame. And out of the darkness of the stable I saw a horse appear, pulling a black carriage. A hooded figure hunched forward on the seat at the front slowly and silently steered the horse out of the courtyard and into the night.

The watchman? It had to be, didn't it? My theory that the vampire we sought was in fact a member of the royal court, if not the prince himself, was right. He was creeping out in the dead of night to kill his next victim, another young girl he should have been watching over.

With heart racing, I flicked the cigarette into the fire grate and went to pull on my dress.

"Harry," I said, reaching out and shaking his shoulder. "Harry, wake up."

He groaned in his sleep and rolled over.

"Harry, I think I was right about the watchman after all. It is someone close to the king and they're on their way to take another victim . . ." I stopped, looking at Harry as he lay deep in sleep on the bed.

How can we believe in you when you don't believe in yourself, I heard Zoe's voice rattle about my brain.

Maybe that was the whole point – the point Zoe and my friends were trying to make. I would never stay with the preacher, Harry, Louise and Zoe because I didn't really believe in them. To me they had just been part of a fantasy, one you could dip in and out of whenever you wanted. A fantasy you could easily forget. If I wanted to stay then I had to believe not only in my friends but in myself too. I believed the watchman – the vampire – was Prince James. I just had to have a little faith in myself that I was right. If I could do that, then I would stay with my friends – with Harry.

I snatched up Harry's cloak and threw it on. At the door, I pulled the hood up over my head and sneaked out of the room in pursuit of the watchman.

30

With the cloak wrapped tight about me I cut across the courtyard like a shadow, making for the stables. At the door, I kept low and peered inside. I took short shallow breaths and willed my heart not to beat so fast. The stableman I had seen before was not about. Sleeping, I guessed, in one of the other stables, buried beneath a pile of hay and picking the seat of his pants from his arse. Making sure I wasn't being watched, I eased open the door and stepped inside. The horse that Louise and I had ridden across London a few nights before was tethered nearby. I went over and stroked it gently on the muzzle.

"Good boy," I whispered. The reins and bridle hung from the stable wall. I placed them over the horse's head, fastening them in place. As the horse pawed the straw-covered floor with one front hoof, I noticed something and lifted its front leg to inspect the hoof more closely. The shoe hadn't been replaced. The stableman had lied to us. But why? Had he been given orders to do so? And for what reason?

To frame my friends – the wolves – for the killings of those young girls.

Knowing I had little time to waste, I mounted the horse and rode it out of the stable, gathering speed as we cleared the palace grounds and headed across St James's Park. I could just make out the carriage on the other side of the park. Once I had it in sight I kept a safe distance, sheltering in the shadows cast by the trees. There was no moon tonight, and the sky was dark with cloud. The fires that burned at regular intervals gave me light in which to see the carriage ahead.

Crouching low over the neck of my horse, I flicked the reins and trotted onwards, always keeping the sleek black carriage in sight. It cleared the park and turned into a narrow side street. I followed. The clop-clop sound of my horse's hooves echoed off the cobbles. Fearing that the driver might hear, I stayed back as far as I dared without losing them. When the carriage turned into another cobbled street, I followed the sound of its own horse's clomping hooves. In some streets the houses on each side were so close that I could've reached out and touched their overhanging fronts. But the meaner the streets were the thicker the smoke that filled them. At times it swirled around me like an impenetrable fog, and I lost sight of the carriage ahead. The smoke was so dense that even the sound of the horse's hooves on the uneven road surface became muffled to near-silence.

People cried out from their houses, their bodies feverish with the plague, death awaiting them. So many doors had been branded with a red cross on them and the stench of rotting bodies was putrid. I covered my nose. With the eerie glow of the flickering fires, the swirling smog and the moans of pain, I guessed that this was what hell must be like. Then over the sound of the dying I heard another noise, like scampering from above. I glanced up. The noise came again. Shadows flitting over the roofs of the nearby houses. Vampires? Perhaps I should have woken Harry? Perhaps I should've been more insistent with the preacher and demanded that he believe me. Now I heard the sound of running, like someone or something was racing over the roofs.

Suddenly I pulled sharply on the reins. My horse neighed and tossed its giant head from side to side as I brought the creature to an abrupt halt. The carriage had stopped. It stood in the dark amongst the churning smog outside one of the terraced houses. From the shadows I watched the carriage door slowly open. A figure dressed in long dark robes with the hood up climbed out. Whoever it was spoke to the driver but I was too far away to hear what was said. The driver then cracked his whip and the carriage moved slowly on, where I lost sight of it in the smoke-ridden street. The hooded figure stood gazing up at one of the bedroom windows. A light flickered on and the pale face of a girl appeared behind the grubby windowpane. No sooner had she appeared than she was gone again and the front door was swinging open. The hooded figure stepped inside, closing the door behind it.

I sat in the dark not knowing what to do. Should I go and check the house out? Peer through one of the downstairs windows in the hope I might see the hooded figure reveal himself? Wait for the carriage to come back and follow it again? Should I—

A heart-stopping scream came from the house. I prodded the horse's flanks and shot forward towards it as the shadows flitted above me again. It was like the terrified scream had excited them somehow. Outside the house I sprang from the horse, the tails of my cloak flapping around me like wings.

The scream came again, fading out into a series of gurgling sobs. I pushed open the door with my shoulder. The house was in near-darkness, just a few scattered candles giving light. I could hear the sound of tearing fabric – or was that flesh – from above. I instantly reached beneath my cloak for a stake. Wrong costume. I was wearing the dress the king had given me. I searched the pockets of my cloak for my rosary beads. Wrong cloak. It was Harry's. I had nothing to defend myself against the vampire I now feared was devouring the girl upstairs. I was out of weapons, out of luck and now it looked as if I was out of time.

I hurtled up the stairs and on to a landing, looking in the direction of the gut-wrenching sound of ripping and tearing. It was louder up here – deafening. The noises were coming from behind a door at the opposite end of the landing. I charged forward, barging it open. At the open doorway I threw my hands to my face in horror. Blood ran down the dirty walls in thick maroon rivulets. Flesh and entrails coiled like black snakes over the wooden floorboards. The sheets on the bed were stained crimson as the naked girl lay dead and half devoured. The hooded figure I had seen enter the house was bent forward, head buried deep in guts. The sound of slurping and chewing was maddening. I felt as if I were losing my fucking mind.

Without thinking I grabbed the figure's cloak in my fists. I just wanted those disgusting sounds to stop, wanted him to stop eating that girl. The figure must have felt me on him as he lurched backwards, shoving me into one of the blood-soaked walls. Beneath the darkness of the hood I saw a set of red eyes blazing like two pools of lava. I launched myself at the stranger, pulling his hood back, then looked into his face and screamed. Not out of fear but from shock at who was now staring back at me.

"You?" I whispered.

The vampire screamed, its bloody mouth stretching wide across its face like that of a deformed clown. With stringy strips of the girl's flesh hanging from its spiked teeth the creature lunged at me.

31

The vampire's claws were just inches from my throat when the bedroom window shattered inwards in a spray of broken glass. I looked up and so did the vampire to see the preacher come bounding through the window, his own giant claws raised and eyes ablaze. Zoe came hurtling through after him and Harry and Louise came bursting through the bedroom door. The four of them dived in front of me, Harry striking out with his long ragged claws, sending the vampire sprawling back across the room into the wall. The house seemed to shake. Masonry and dust fell down from the force of the vampire smashing into the wall.

"Your fight isn't with Sammy, Majesty," the preacher said. "It's with us, the Skinturners."

The vampire sprang to its feet and stood before us. I

watched as its face contorted and twisted back into its human form. My heart felt like breaking as I stared at the queen.

"Why?" I asked, looking into her pretty face. She no longer looked sad, but happy.

Before the queen had a chance to answer, someone else entered the room.

We all turned to see Prince James standing in the open doorway, a musket pressed into his shoulder and aimed at us. He glanced down at my friends' swinging paws, then up at their hair-covered faces. "If one of you so much as twitches, I'll blow your filthy wolf heads clean off," he said.

The queen, now looking very human, subtly wiped the last of the girl's blood from her chin. She threw her hands to her face. "Thank goodness you came, James. They were just about to kill me like they have this poor girl." She waved in the direction of the bed, as if too horrified by the sight to look at it. "They kidnapped me and brought here. They wanted to sacrifice me. Once they had killed me they were going to come after you and the king. They want us all dead."

The sadness I had once seen in the queen's eyes had now been replaced with cunning.

"It was you all along?" A part of me still too unwilling to believe that she was the one who had killed the young girls.

The queen looked at me, her eyes now black. Placing

one arm against her brow, she cried out, then fainted down on to the floor. It was all very dramatic but I wasn't going to be fooled by her again. I darted forward, wanting to yank her to her feet, to prove that this was just an act. I wanted to hear her confess before the prince.

"Get back!" he roared, aiming the gun at me. "All of you will hang for this. I knew my brother was foolish to trust you. I told him it was you who had brought the plague to London. I told him it was you who were eating the dead just like the filthy wolves I can now see that you truly are."

"You're wrong about us," the preacher said. "We came here to help you. To save you from creatures like your queen."

"Guards!" the prince bellowed, ignoring my friend.

Instantly we were joined in the blood-stained room by several guards wearing those crimson tunics and round black hats. Each of them carried a musket like the prince. One of them looked down at the bed where the half-eaten girl lay in a black sticky pool of her own blood. His face drained white and for a moment I thought he might faint just like the queen, although I suspected his fainting would be for real and not a ruse to trick the prince.

"Take the queen to my carriage and shackle these animals," the prince ordered.

"You don't want to take the queen back to the palace," the preacher tried to warn James.

The angry prince stood in front of the preacher. "I will

not take orders from a filthy animal like you." Then with a sharp snorting noise he spat a mouthful of snot into the preacher's face. It ran down his nose and dropped on to his bushy moustache.

"Hey, back off!" Zoe objected, stepping between the preacher and the prince as if to protect her friend. For someone so delicate-looking she had guts and was fiercely loyal to her friends. They were her family – her pack – she had told me that. "How did I ever think a guy who swaggers around in a wig could be hot?"

"Get these animals out of here," the prince sneered.

The guards lowered their muskets and came to shackle our hands behind our backs with thick chains. As they secured me, I watched two of them scoop the queen up from the floor and reverently carry her from the room.

We were pushed and shoved from behind as we were forced down the stairs and out into the street. It was still dark and smoky outside. The queen was being eased into the prince's carriage. There was another carriage, but this had bars on the back door. We were manhandled into it and pushed down on to the filthy floor. The chains cut into my wrists and I couldn't help but cry out.

"Are you okay?"

I looked up to see Harry beside me.

"I've felt better," I said.

"You know we're really in the shit this time," Zoe said, as she tried to sit up and make herself as comfortable as she could in the confines of the carriage.

"What's new," Louise said.

Did they have a plan? I hoped so.

The preacher said nothing. It was then a thought struck me. "What are you all doing here anyhow? I left Harry snoring in bed at the palace and you were meant to be staking the dead."

"We followed you," the preacher said. "It was always part of the plan."

"Plan? What freaking plan?"

"When you released us from the crypt and told us what you had discovered, we knew that you had probably stumbled upon something . . ."

"But you said you didn't believe me," I reminded him, the prison carriage bumping roughly over the cobbled streets as we were led into the night by the prince and his men.

"Of course we believed you," Louise said. "You're our friend."

I wasn't sure how to feel. Part of me felt angry as if I had been duped somehow, but another part of me felt happy that they considered me their friend and had risked everything to come and save me. "So why did you all give me such a hard time?"

The preacher looked across the rattling carriage at me. "*We* believed but we needed *you* to believe, Sammy. It was my hope that if you had something important here – in 1665 – something you had to prove to yourself, then you might not leave again. I prayed that perhaps you might stay this time. What matters is whether you believe in yourself."

"But I did," I said, my eyes wide. "I believed enough to risk everything and come after the vampire. Do you think I've done enough to stay and not go back?"

"Only you know that," the preacher said. "But it's about remembering too."

"Remembering what?"

"Who and what you really are," he said, cold eyes piercing mine.

"So why don't you just tell me," I said, frustrated.

"Because you wouldn't truly *believe* me even if I did," he said. "And that is why I fear you will go back and leave us again."

While I was trying to make sense of what he had told me, the carriage came to a juddering stop. The door was flung open and we were grabbed by the guards. I was hauled out, pain exploding in my shoulders as I was dragged across the courtyard into the palace and, I suspected, the presence of the waiting king.

32

The room we were led into was different from the room where I had first met the king. There was no long table or other furnishings, just two thrones, side by side at the far end. The king sat in one, his queen next to him in the other. Her eyes never left mine as we were shoved towards them. At once I looked about for any way of escape or weapon. There were two long windows on my left and two swords hung on the wall behind the thrones. Their razor-sharp blades gleamed in the twitching candlelight. Even if I could have reached them, my hands were secured firmly behind my back.

My friends walked on either side of me towards the king and queen, Harry and Zoe to my right, Louise and the preacher to my left. And even though we were undoubtedly facing death, for the first time I felt a part of something:

part of the pack. But that feeling didn't seem so unfamiliar. It was like I had felt it before. Perhaps now as my life drew to an end I was finally beginning to remember. Just my kind of luck.

The guards ordered us to stop. We were standing about six feet before the king. He was dressed in the same clothes I had seen him wearing earlier that night as he had thrust his cock against my stomach while we danced. His long curly wig flowed down over his shoulders. The queen's hair was pulled up now, but she still wore the velvet trousers and white blouse as before. The blood-soaked cloak was missing so none of her clothes had been stained with blood. There was no clue that she had been responsible for that girl's death and as to what she really was or had done. A cruel smile curled at the corners of her mouth.

The prince stopped before us and looked at the king. "I told you not to trust the preacher and his people. He is not an agent of God, but the Devil."

The king looked at the preacher and I was sure I saw disappointment in his stare. "Is this true?"

"No," the preacher said.

"I thought you served me," he said. "I am your king, am I not?"

"I only serve one king," the preacher said, never breaking the king's stare. "His crown wasn't made of gold but thorns."

"And he didn't wear a wig," Harry cut in.

"Stop this insolence!" James roared, striding forwards and striking Harry across the face with the back of his hand. His head rocked to the right, a thin trail of blood leaking from his nose and on to his top lip. The queen's chest heaved up and down and knew she had caught the sudden scent.

"It is not only I who do not follow you," the preacher said. "Your queen also follows a different king."

"And what is this king's name? From what country does he hail?" the king scoffed.

"He calls himself the Pale Liege and he comes from hell," the preacher said.

"You lie!" the queen shouted. Even the king seemed surprised by this sudden explosion of anger. "It is you who come from hell. James and I saw your claws and how your faces had changed. All of you looked like hounds – hounds from hell."

"Is this true?" the king asked his brother.

"Yes," the prince said. "They looked like wolves that walked upright on two legs. Just like the rumours I told you about."

"And where did these rumours start?" I said. All eyes turned to me as if I'd been forgotten up until that moment. The king looked down at me from his throne. "The queen started these rumours as she knew this moment would one day come. If you tell a lie often enough, it becomes the truth."

"You don't know what you're saying," the queen started up again.

"It was you who killed and ate those young girls," I said. "It has been you who spread the plague."

"What is this nonsense?" the queen spat, now standing up.

"It was you who brought the plague to these shores," the preacher stated. "You brought it on the boat you sailed from Portugal. You carried it in your bite, in the blood that surges through your veins. You bit the ship's rats, infected them with your venom knowing that they would scurry ashore when arriving in the London docks. They would do your work for you while you settled into your new life and home. And when the plague started to spread, people would blame the vermin, while your kind fed on the flesh of the dead who were cast into the death pits. With every mouthful your kind grew stronger. But they wanted more – you wanted more. You wanted to eat and drink the flesh of the living."

"This is ridiculous," the queen scoffed. "I was kidnapped by these animals tonight after escorting this girl here to her room. They lay in wait for me there and smuggled me away into the night. They took me to that house where there was a poor wretched girl who looked as if she had been devoured in some way."

The king looked at the queen then back at his brother as if for help and guidance. The queen noticed this and cut in. "They took me there in the carriage the stableman had given to them. We've all heard the rumours that a carriage has been seen near to where these poor girls have died."

I knew then that it had been the queen who had given the order for our horses to be taken and replaced with the carriage. I had been right, we had been set up.

"We couldn't have taken you anywhere in that carriage tonight," Louise said. "It was ripped to pieces the other night when we were attacked by some of your friends."

"What are you talking about?" the king blustered. "None of this is making sense."

"Ask your queen to explain it," Zoe said.

"There is nothing to explain," the queen said with a confident smile. "The witnesses maintain they all saw a man leave the houses where those poor girls were eaten."

"They only *thought* they saw a man," I countered. "That is the real reason you dress differently from other women in the court. They all wear dresses and you choose to wear trousers and shirts just like a . . . like a man."

"Do you really think I would want to dress anything like that woman Castlemaine?" the queen sneered. "Why, she may as well not wear anything at all from the waist up."

The king shifted in his seat, as if ready to defend his mistress.

Mistress! The word screamed across the front of my mind like a bunch of neon lights above a bar. "That's why you didn't mind the king having a mistress," I began as it all started to make sense. "You were pleased that the king never came to your bed because it left you free to sneak away at night and—"

"Stop this!" the king demanded. "Enough! You can't prove a word of this and I should have had you beheaded for treason already."

The only way of proving I was telling the truth would be to force the queen to reveal what she truly was. I was right out of holy water, garlic, and crucifixes. "Go and fetch the stableman," I said to the king. "Ask him in what state we brought the carriage back tonight and who it was who gave him the order to take our horses away and replace them with a carriage."

The king looked at me, then at his brother and finally at his queen.

"Take off her head!" she roared at him.

He flinched. "Bring the stableman to me," he ordered one of his guards.

The guard nodded and marched from the room.

"You believe her before your queen?" the queen screeched. "It is no surprise to me, you put all women before me." Then she snatched one of the swords from the wall. "I will prove once and for all who the liar is. I will take off her head."

The queen sprang towards me, closing the gap with frightening speed. She gripped my hair in one fist, holding the sword aloft in the other, dragging me around so she was behind me, then forcing me down on to my knees. I tried to struggle free from her grip, but with my hands chained behind my back it was impossible. She pushed my head down, and pulled back my hair to reveal the nape of my neck. It was then she started to scream.

I heard the sword clatter to the floor, the sound of her hissing and spitting in the back of her throat. I turned my head to see her throw her hands over her eyes. It was like she had seen something on the back of my neck which had terrified her in some way. I shot a look at the preacher, then Zoe and Louise. None of them seemed to be surprised by the queen's sudden and violent convulsions. I looked at Harry.

"Paris," he said, then winked back at me.

Paris! Why did he keeping going on about freaking Paris. What had happened there?

The queen screamed as tendrils of smoke seeped from her skin. It looked as if she was going to burst into flames at any moment. Her flesh began to crack and blister as if she were being turned on a spit. The prince staggered backwards, his mouth open and eyes bulging. The king shot from his throne and took cover behind it.

"Cut us loose! Cut us loose!" the preacher shouted.

The king poked his head around the side of his throne.

"Have we not proved to you that it is not we who are your enemy, but this queen?" Harry roared at the king, struggling against his restraints.

"Do you not see that this is not your queen, Majesty, but that of another?" Louise tried to reason with him.

The queen threw herself about the room. Her mouth stretched open, so wide it looked as if the lower half of her face was tearing apart. Sharpened teeth gnashed as she opened and closed her mouth.

The king watched this change as he cowered. "For God's sake release the preacher and his people!" he finally commanded. "Do it, little brother, before this devil kills us all."

James turned to his guards and barked, "Do as the king says and set these people free."

The guards came and released the chains that held us prisoner. As soon as my hands were free, I reached up and ran my fingertips over the nape of my neck, desperate to know what it was the queen had seen. I gently brushed my fingers over the skin and flinched away. The skin was raised, feeling like an old burn in the shape of a cross. I heard Harry's chains clatter to the floor and looked in his direction.

"Paris?" I asked him.

"Put the weapons down," someone shouted.

The guard who had been sent to fetch the stableman was standing in the open doorway, hands raised above his head. The stableman stepped out from behind him with the guard's musket held in a long pointed set of claws. A wide jagged smile split his face.

Seeing his hideous grin, the other guards dropped their muskets and raised their hands.

"Catherine," the young vampire called out to the queen. "Come to me. It is not too late for you."

The queen staggered blindly in the direction of his voice

and I knew then that they had been working together. The stableman had been the driver of the carriage that she took at night to go eat her victims.

She dropped into his arms and he caught her. Throwing the gun to one side, he scooped her up then sprang into the air, crashing through the window and into the night. I ran and looked out. The vampire was placing the queen into the back of a waiting carriage. He climbed on top and, whipping the horse's reins, steered the carriage across the courtyard and sped away from the palace.

"Where will they go?" the prince asked, sounding breathless and in shock.

"He will take the queen back to their nest," the preacher said. "That will be the safest place for her until she heals."

"Nest?" the king asked, still behind his throne. "What's a nest?"

"A gathering of vampires who are waiting to attack," Zoe said.

"Attack who?" He sounded unsure whether it was safe for him to venture out.

"You," Louise said, taking some delight in telling him.

"Where is this nest?" the prince demanded, snatching up his musket from the floor as if readying himself for battle.

"I guess we won't know unless we follow the queen and the stableman," the preacher said.

"Then what are we waiting for?" the prince bellowed.

"For this," Zoe said striding forward and driving her knee deep between the prince's legs.

"What was that for?" the prince cried out, dropping to the floor.

"Spitting in the preacher's face," she told him. "No one treats the man I love as a father like that."

The king came out from behind his throne now that the danger had gone. He looked at his brother writhing on the floor, then up at us. "Well, don't delay. I order you to go after those creatures and protect me and my kingdom."

"Order, you say?" I said, coming forward.

"Are you deaf?" he asked, as if trying to regain control over his subjects – over me.

Without answering, I rocked my head back, then brought my forehead smashing down on to the bridge of his nose. I heard it crunch.

The king threw his hands to his nose, dropping to his knees.

"What was that for?" he screamed, thick streams of hot blood pumping through his fingers.

"For grabbing my arse," I said as I left.

33

In the courtyard, no longer fearing their real identities being discovered by the king or anyone else, both the preacher and Harry clawed free of their cloaks and then their clothes. Their faces and muscular bodies bristled with fur. They stood upright, seemingly taller. They had not turned completely, but enough for them to look like a cross between man and wolf – a creature that could still be reasoned with. I looked at Louise and Zoe. They too were now naked apart from the sleek fur that covered them from head to foot. Their facial features were still recognisable and, in a strange kind of way, they looked as beautiful as ever – if not more. They stood, slightly stooped as if their giant paws were pulling each of them forward.

Throwing his head back the preacher howled up into

the night sky, his eyes burning bright in the dark. Without saying anything the four of them tore across the courtyard after the fleeing carriage.

"Wait for me!" I hollered.

I ran to the stable and mounted the first horse I could see, then rode out beneath the archway, past the turrets and across St James's Park. I could see the wolves bounding ahead of me as the carriage fled into the night. The horse galloped after them. The cold night wind blasted into my face, throwing up flakes of powdery ash. The smoke stung my eyes and I felt grit sting my skin like needlepoints. I snatched at the back of my hood, pulling it low over my face as I charged onward.

I drew level with my friends and they bounded along on either side of me. Louise and Zoe ran upright, only dropping down every now and then as if to propel themselves forward with the aid of their claws. The preacher and Harry loped on all fours; long hair now streaming back from their faces, arms and legs. Harry glanced back at me as he streaked along. His eyes burned a fierce yellow, like two seething suns. He howled, revealing the jagged teeth now standing like blades in his gums.

We cleared the park and were soon navigating the narrow winding streets that covered so much of London. Beside me I could hear the wolves panting and howling over the sound of my horse's hooves on the cobbles. The carriage was ahead of us looking like an ancient hearse. I drove the horse harder and faster. The carriage lurched right, taking a sharp bend in the road. I thought it was going to tip over as two of the wheels rose up from off the street but it righted itself again, shaking as it crashed back to the ground and moved on.

Through the swirling smoke, I could see the banks of the River Thames. Barges and ships sounded their foghorns in the smog that floated across its dark waters. The carriage sped alongside the river and we followed. The preacher was ahead of us now, his sleek silver fur gleaming in the firelight. Within touching distance of the carriage and the vampire queen, the preacher leapt into the air. Something else sprang across my eye line, shooting through the smoke in a black blur, and crashed into the preacher. He shot sideways through the night, clattering into the road. Dazed, he shook his head from side to side. Once he had regained his senses, the preacher howled, gnashing his jaws at the vampire which had leapt from the shore of the river. Then, as if they were somehow dropping out of the night sky, we suddenly came under attack from a group of vampires. Their faces screwed tight with hate, they screeched and hissed, slashing the night sky apart with their long pointed claws. The preacher lunged for them as did Harry, Louise and Zoe. The violence between them was ferocious and bloody as they clashed. Ahead I could see the carriage disappearing into the smoke.

I heard the sickening sound of slobbering and saw Zoe burying her fangs into the neck of a vampire that thrashed angrily beneath her. Zoe spat its face free. Howling, she sprang on to the back of another. Louise suddenly leapt from out of the smoke, her claws sinking into the throat of a vampire. She dragged it back under and I lost sight of them beneath the rolling sea of fog. I heard the vampire screech, then fall silent. This was followed by the sound of chomping jaws and bones breaking. Meanwhile Harry was dragging his powerful-looking claws across the midriff of a vampire he had hold of. The vampire's intestines spilled over Harry's claws like a nest of vipers. Harry noticed me watching him from my horse. As if wanting to hide his butchery from me, he turned the vampire around.

"Sammy!" I heard someone roar.

The preacher was looking out of the smoke. The fur covering his forearms was drenched black with blood, and a vampire's head swung from his fist. He wiped blood and flesh from his mouth. "We've got everything under control here. Go after the carriage, see where it stops and then come back for us. We need to find the nest."

"But—" I started.

"Go!" he ordered me.

Without another word of protest, I charged after the carriage. I hadn't been reluctant to do so out of fear for myself; I didn't want to leave my friends to fight the vampires alone. Glancing back just once, I saw the preacher disappear again deep within the smoke. The sounds of vampires crying out in pain was so loud, it muffled the noise of the barges and ships using their horns on the river. Then I galloped after the carriage.

I could just make it out ahead, like some ghostly apparition floating in and out of the churning smoke and wavering firelight as if it was carrying the dead into hell. It began to slow, and I dropped back out of sight. I watched as the stableman stood in his seat atop the carriage and checked for danger. He waited and when no wolves came bounding out of the smoke he moved off again. At a safe distance I followed as the stableman steered the carriage into another side street. Not knowing exactly where I was and fearing I might never find my way back to my friends and then lead them here, I looked for any landmark I might later use as a guide. There was a sign attached to a nearby wall, the name of the street I now found myself in: Pudding Lane.

This was the place where the Great Fire of London would start next year in 1666. I wasn't really surprised that most of London eventually burnt down with so many fires blazing night and day in the streets. The carriage came to a stop ahead of me. The stableman climbed down from his seat and went to the side of the carriage where he opened the door and leant inside. Moments later he reappeared carrying the queen in his arms. He took her across the street and into a building that from the front looked no larger than a small house. Should I go back to my friends now? Or perhaps wait and make sure this was the place where the vampires had built their nest? What if I led my friends back here only to find the carriage and the queen gone again? What if this was a trap set by the stableman? He could be waiting in that building, keeping watch to see if they were being followed after all. Then again they could be getting away via some tunnel or other passageway at the back of the building.

With my heart beginning to quicken, I dismounted from the horse and stole through the darkness towards the building. From the shadow of a nearby doorway I glanced up at a small wooden sign above the door. It read, *Bakery*. Why would the stableman take the queen to a bakery? It had to be some kind of ruse. They had escaped me somehow. After looking left, then right, I approached the door and slowly went inside.

34

The smell of freshly baked bread wafted beneath my nose and made my mouth water. It was the nicest aroma I had smelt since arriving in 1665. Large furnaces were fixed into the bare brick walls that surrounded me. Light glowed from around the edges of the giant doors, an intense heat leaking from them. I could see long wooden tables covered in a dusty layer of flour. This was where the dough for the bread must have been rolled, I thought, heading deeper and deeper into the bakery. The intoxicating smell enticed me forward, my stomach now somersaulting with a sudden hunger.

There was a noise ahead of me, like whispering voices in the dark. I inched over the stone floor, careful not to make a sound. Was it the vampire queen and the stableman I could hear talking? At the back of the bakery all I discovered was a wall. The muffled voices seemed louder now. Were they coming from the other side of the wall? I could see no door – not even a secret one. Then at a noise from behind me I turned to see a trapdoor swing up and open in the floor of the bakery. The stableman poked out his head and looked as surprised to see me as I was him. He shot his hand out, gripping my ankle. With one sharp tug I was falling, the back of my head smashing into the stone floor. There was a sickening crack and the world swam before me.

Come back, Sammy! I heard someone shout.

Harry the paramedic was leaning over me again.

Stand clear! he roared, driving his fist down on to my chest as if trying to restart my heart.

Then he was gone and I was being dragged across the bakery floor and into the opening. My head slammed into every one of the steps leading down into the dark depths. By the time the stableman had manhandled me to the bottom of the stairs, my head felt like it had been repeatedly struck with a sledgehammer. He pulled me to my feet and I wobbled from side to side.

A light flickered in the dark ahead of me. As it grew nearer, the stableman gripped me from behind, blocking my only way of escape back up the stairs. The light stopped just before me. In the torchlight I could see the blistered face of the queen; it looked melted in parts, like wax dripping down the side of a candle.

"Don't look so alarmed, Samantha Carter, my face will

soon heal, unlike yours." She reached out with one hooked finger and sliced the jagged fingernail down the length of my left cheek. I felt it open like ripe fruit skin and cried out in pain as hot blood trickled down my face and along the curve of my jaw.

"You are not a Skinturner although you run with a pack of them," the queen said, her eyes white and pupilless. "But he could make you look beautiful again."

"Who?" I said, with a flash of red hot pain every time I opened my mouth to speak.

"The Pale Liege. Just like King Charles, my king favours many lovers. Why don't you join us, Samantha. He could make us both feel beautiful again."

"So is your king here?" I asked, scanning the darkness. In the pale glow of her torch I could see more of those furnaces set into the walls. But unlike the ones I had seen upstairs in the bakery, there was no fire behind them, nor any heat. Only cold leaked from them, like a draught was blowing up deep from below ground.

"He isn't here yet," the queen said. "But it is only a matter of time."

"So if I wanted to go to your king now, if I wanted him to make me beautiful again, could you take me to him?" I asked, gingerly placing my fingertips to my bloodied cheek.

"You would have to be welcomed into the nest first," she said, a sly smile forming around the edges of her blistered, split lips.

"Where is the nest?" I asked, fearing I was standing in the very heart of it. She had no intention of welcoming me to the nest or taking me to her king. I had the mark of the cross on my neck. She had cut my cheek to draw blood and entice the vampires out to feed one last time before they went above ground and took London.

As if reading my mind, she said, "Sammy, you know this is the nest."

Beyond her I saw those furnace doors open. I watched in horror as white bodies climbed from behind them. The vampires who now emerged looked as if they were yet to properly form. They were painfully thin, their bones jutting through their paper-thin flesh. Their heads were narrow and bald, some so misshapen they were unrecognisable as skulls. Others made a mewing noise in the backs of their throats as they staggered forward seeking out food – blindly following the scent of the fresh blood running from my cheek. The cellar I was now trapped in was soon filled with twisting and twitching bodies of vampires who had slithered from the makeshift furnaces.

With my survival senses as raw as the pain in my cheek, I cast my eyes about, looking for any weapon I might be able to use to make an escape. I saw one: the queen was holding it. In one swift movement I rocked my head back, driving my skull into the face of the stableman standing behind me. As he flew backwards I reached out, snatching the torch from the queen's hand. With the stableman screaming in pain, I lunged at the queen, driving the flaming torch into her face.

Screeching, she stumbled away, a black charred hole in the centre of her face. Flames leapt over her already dry and blistered skin. They caught hold of her hair, making it go up in a plume of flame and smoke. Frantically, she slapped at her face and head with her hands, desperate to put out the fire that now engulfed her head. She staggered wildly about, knocking into the mutant-looking vampires that had clambered free from the furnaces, some still so weak and malformed that they fell over, taking more of the creatures with them. The queen ran around in blind circles; as she went, I lit the frills of her shirt. The flames ran greedily up her arms and across her chest. She shrieked so loud I thought my eardrums might just burst. The sickly sweet smell of burning flesh now masked the scent of freshly baked bread. The queen reeled towards the wooden stairs leading to the bakery but collapsed halfway up.

I felt hands grab at my legs and looked down to see the stableman clawing at my shin. The lower half of his face was covered red with the thick clots of blood that pumped from his broken nose. I drove the heel of my shoe into his upturned face and he fell away, blood spraying in a wide arc from his lips. Some of those half-formed vampires caught a whiff of that fresh blood and within seconds I had lost sight of him beneath the mass of sickly white bodies that now covered him. Over the noise of crackling flames I heard the sound of gnawing and gobbling as they ate one of their own.

I wanted to make my escape, but there was no way out for me. The flames that danced over the queen's still body had now engulfed the stairs and were scampering over the ceiling and the hatch I would need to escape through. As the fire rapidly spread throughout the cellar, my skin began to prickle with heat and my throat became clogged with suffocating smoke. My lungs tightened in my chest as I tried not to breathe in the clouds of burning hot fumes. But it was impossible not to do so. Some of those grotesque-looking vampires caught fire as the wooden beams holding up the roof dropped upon them, riddled with scorching flames.

Over the fire's din, I thought I heard someone shout my name. I looked up, tears streaming from my smoke-filled eyes. Flames now took hold of my cloak and scurried up me, the pain unbearable. The sound of someone calling my name came again.

Through the smoke I made out that the burning hatch had been thrown open and my friends stood staring down at me. My heart leapt.

"Sammy!" Harry was shouting. "Sammy, come back!" He held out his hand for me to take but it was impossible.

The preacher knew that too as he pulled Harry back from the inferno.

In the fire that raged, I knew that the nest and the vampires hatching within it had been destroyed. I looked up once more at Harry. His eyes met mine. *When will I see you again?* I wondered as the flames took me.

35

The sound of the fire alarm was almost deafening; a mechanical voice spoke over it.

"*Due to a reported emergency all passengers must leave the station immediately. Please obey the instructions of the staff. Due to a reported emergency* . . ." The voice was on a pre-recorded loop.

I was shoved from behind, but this time not in front of an approaching train. I was at the bottom of the stairs leading away from the platforms and out of Aldgate Tube Station. I blinked. Was that Harry up there looking down at me just like he had through that burning hole?

The fire: I was burning alive in the basement of a bakery in late November 1665. Harry was there with the preacher, Louise and Zoe, but they couldn't reach me and I couldn't reach them because of the flames . . .

"Fire!" I said out loud.

"There's no need to panic," someone said in my ear.

A member of the Underground staff was ushering me and the other passengers up the stairs and out of the station.

"No, you don't understand," I said, trying to head down the stairs against the flowing tide of passengers all desperate to leave the station. "I have to get back to Harry. He's waiting for me."

"Your friend is probably waiting for you outside the station," the member of staff in the blue tunic said, taking me by the arm. "It's easy to get separated from your friends in a panic."

"You don't understand," I told him again as he guided me up the stairs and on to the concourse. "I have to go back. If I don't, I might forget and never remember . . ."

"You can come back after," he said, pulling the grille over the entrance to the station.

"Please," I said, rattling it with my hands. "You have to let me go down there again."

"Sorry." He shrugged.

In the distance, I could hear the sound of approaching fire engines.

I waited at the kerb in the dark and the drizzle. Some people waited too for the station to reopen; others hailed a cab or boarded a bus. But as I stood and watched the rain bounce off the slick pavement outside the station, I knew that whether I went back in or not it was over again, just like it had been before. I was now dressed in my long black coat, denim jeans and boots. I was here in 2014 and I didn't want to be. Every time I came back I felt a little less connected to the year I believed I came from. What did I have here – not much? In the past I had the preacher, Louise, Zoe and Harry. I had adventure, excitement, love; I had a life.

Pulling the collar of my coat up against the rain, I saw the tower of St Botolph Church, no longer made of wood but of grey stone, like I remembered. I walked down the street towards it. There was no graveyard in front and I guessed no small stable at the back. It was hard for me to comprehend that I had once lived at that church; I'd had a life there with my friends. Tears were burning at the corner of my eyes. I didn't want to go home in case I started to forget. I mustn't do that or I might never go back again. I still had so much to discover about myself. The preacher had said he was going to tell me once we had destroyed the vampires' nest. But he was there and I was here – 349 years between us.

With head down, I walked the wet streets of London. Cabs and busses hissed past in the rain. I walked through the city, not knowing where I was going or why. It was only after some time that I looked up and saw the domed roof of St Paul's in the distance. It was no longer a tall spire. So the Fire of London must have happened or the wooden spire would still have been there.

"The Fire of London," I breathed out loud.

I headed back across London and towards home.

In the hallway, I shook the rain from my coat and listened to the unmistakable sound of Sally getting shagged in her room further down the hallway. I went straight to my room and closed the door. My laptop was still on from early that day; it was like no time had passed at all. I found a pack of cigarettes and lit one, then typed the words *Great Fire of London* into the search engine and hit the return key. It came up with hundreds of results. I hit the first and read the article. And as I read my mouth dropped open and my heart skipped a beat. The Great Fire of London had no longer started on the second of September 1666 but on the fifth of November 1665. How was that possible? I scanned the screen to discover that the fire had started in a bakery in Pudding Lane. That part of history had remained unchanged. What had changed it had been me.

I sat down on the edge of my bed and lit another cigarette. The realisation I had started the fire as I'd tried to kill the queen and the rest of the vampires in the nest kind of left me feeling numb.

Sometimes we change history, I heard Louise say as if she were in the room with me.

Sally cried with joy from further down the hall.

Placing the laptop on the bed, I read the rest of the article. It said the fire raged across London for five days and was believed to be the reason the plague eventually died out. On the third day, King Charles the Second and his brother James had come on to the streets of London and helped the citizens fight the fire back.

Perhaps the king had grown some balls after all.

What of the queen? I wondered, scrolling down. Near to the bottom I read that the queen had disappeared during the Great Fire and it was rumoured that she had fled to her home country of Portugal and was not seen or heard of again. There were other rumours that the king had her beheaded in secret so that he could continue the relationships he had with his many mistresses.

And as I looked at the screen, I knew in my heart it was only I who knew the true fate of Queen Catherine of Braganza. There was no mention of my friends, or any wolves for that matter. I turned the laptop off, lay on my side and fell into a deep and dreamless sleep.

I stood before the bathroom mirror feeling fresh and clean after taking my first shower in what seemed like hundreds of years. As I stared at my reflection, I caught sight of a faint white line running the length of my left cheek. It looked like an ancient scar long since healed and now faded. I knew what it was and I hoped I would never forget how I had come by it. Drying my hair, I let my fingers deliberately brush over the nape of my neck. The skin felt raised there, like I had once been burnt, the mark of a crucifix permanently branded there. I let my hair fall back into place, but I checked it each morning, so that I wouldn't forget.

Over the next weeks and months, I wrote down

everything I could remember from my time spent in 1665. Every detail, so if I ever started to feel that I was forgetting I could turn to my notes. I carried them with me everywhere. They became my Bible. I made other inquiries too. I telephoned London Ambulance Headquarters and asked if they had anyone working for them with the name of Harry Turner. The young woman on the end of the phone told me she couldn't possibly give me such information as it would be a breach of data protection. It was worth the try though. How else would I discover if Harry was moonlighting as a paramedic? Buy a motorbike and become an ambulance chaser? No. Although every time I heard the sounds of sirens I did glance up – you know – just in case. I even thought about faking a heart attack and dialling 999 – but I soon pushed those crazy thoughts from my mind.

Still, there was one thing that just went around and around in my head and I thought of it every morning when I washed my hair and felt that burn in the shape of a cross. Harry had told me that we had once been together in Paris. As far as I was aware I had never been there. So over the next few months I saved enough money from my new part-time job as a cleaner at Aldgate Tube Station (I liked to hang out there as much as possible – so why not get paid too) and booked myself an online ticket to travel to Paris by Eurostar. I also booked myself into a cheap hotel for two nights. It was all I could afford.

As I stood in line, rucksack over my shoulder, I hoped

that my trip to Paris might spark a memory – a clue – that would lead me back to Harry and my friends. I reached the ticket counter and gave the guy behind it my reference number. He printed out my ticket, placed it in an envelope and handed it to me.

"Have a pleasant journey," he said with a smile.

"I hope so." I smiled back. When I saw the ticket, however, I frowned. "There must be some kind of mistake. This ticket is for business class. The one I paid for was standard class. I couldn't afford to travel business."

"Let me check for you," he said, pressing some keys on the computer. "It looks like someone paid for an upgrade for you this morning."

"Really?" My heart thumped. "What name?"

The ticket seller looked down at the screen then back at me. "A Mr. Harrison Turner," he said.

My hands began to shake. Not through fear, but anticipation. Was it Harry? Was I going back? And if so – where to this time?

"Thank you," I said to the ticket seller.

I stepped on to St Pancras Station concourse and headed for the Eurostar departures. On the way I passed a busker who was strumming on his guitar and singing the song "Bad Moon Rising" by John Fogerty. I stopped and dropped some coins into his guitar case that lay open on the floor.

"Thanks sweetheart." He winked at me, then continued singing.

I walked away, the song ringing in my ears.

At departures, I was ushered through business class like I was royalty. My rucksack was X-rayed, then returned to me. On the departure boards I could see my train was leaving from platform two. I headed up the ramp leading to it; as I went, I checked the face of every man I passed in the hope that one of them might be Harry. I made my way along the platform, the train gleaming white and yellow beside me. The ticket inspector was a young girl who stood waiting by the door to the business-class carriage.

"Have a pleasant journey," she said after checking my ticket.

"I hope so," I said, looking back along the platform before boarding. There was no sign of him.

The carriage door hissed as it slid open. Fortunately my seat was by the window so I could keep an eye on the platform. I waited, strumming my hands on the table before me, but there was no sign of Harry. The platform whistle was blown and the doors to the train were closed. With my nose touching the window, I searched one last time in the hope that Harry might show up.

The train began to move and my heart sank a little. I dropped back in my seat as the train left the station, glancing along the aisle just in case he was seated at some other table in the carriage. But it appeared I was the only person travelling in business class to Paris today.

Leaving London behind, the train raced across the Kent

countryside. Perhaps Harry would be waiting in Paris for me? I hoped so. Out of the window I could see the mouth of the Channel Tunnel in the distance, a giant black hole in the landscape. As we entered it, the door to my carriage slid open. I looked up to see who had joined me. The lights flickered in the carriage and then went out.

Everything went black, masking the face of whoever it was who had come into the carriage and sat down in the seat beside me.

"Harry?" I said.

Want to find out what happened in Paris?
Turn the page for the exclusive short story

VAMPIRE FLAPPERS

For Lynda . . . I will take you to
Paris . . . I promise!

London, 9 November 2013

I couldn't put up with the shrieks of pleasure coming from Sally's room any longer. For two years now we had shared together and for the last year the moans and groans emanating from her room had become too much to bear. Was I jealous? Hell, yeah. Who wouldn't be? Month after month, week after week, day after day, I watched her parade a stream of fit young men into her bedroom. Most were cops. Sally had a *thing* for cops. Like me, she was studying criminology at the University of London so she often listened to those cops' loose lips before, during and after sex. She would suck details about unsolved crimes and on-going investigations from them. Sally always seemed to be sucking one way or another. Christ, she was like a freaking vampire. But at least the vampires only fed off their victims at night – she was at it all day long given half the chance.

But there I go again. Vampires! I knew it wouldn't be too long before my mind rattled back to them. For as long as I can remember I've believed in their existence. Some believe in Santa and the tooth fairy and elves that come out at night and fix your shoes – I believe in vampires. I have every right to believe too. I've seen them. I killed one in a mine back in Colorado of 1888. He was a serial killer – Spencer Drake – a police sergeant from Scotland Yard. Drake was Jack the Ripper. I had to keep reminding myself about him constantly, lest I forget everything.

It had been a year since I came back from November 1888 to November 2012 and with each passing moment, the memories of what happened to me were fading. It was like someone was smearing Vaseline over a window-pane I was desperately trying to stare through. But it wasn't the vampire, Spencer Drake, I feared I would forget, it was the friends I made back there: the preacher and his lover, Louise Pearson, the young and beautiful Zoe Edgar, and . . . and *Harry*. Harry Turner. It was him I so desperately struggled to remember. Even though he was an arrogant jerk, we had shared something. Not just the best sex I had ever had; he was different. How can I explain? He was a werewolf. See, I said it. And did it make me sound crazy? Yes. It made me sound like I lost my freaking mind. How did I possibly travel back in time to Colorado in 1888 and make friends with a group of vampire seekers who themselves happened to be a pack of ferocious werewolves? Oh, and dare I forget, I killed the most famous serial killer of them all. You couldn't make that kinda shit up. Although I must have, or it really happened.

So, as I took shelter from the rain outside Aldgate Tube Station, I dropped the butt of my cigarette into the puddle at my feet and lit another instantly. I was working my way through three packs a day now – the constant flow of nicotine kept my mind focused and it kept me remembering. It kept me awake. I had come to fear sleep. For when I closed my eyes I saw the preacher floating out of the darkness, his long silver pistols gleaming white like the thick droopy moustache that covered his upper lip. Sometimes when I screwed my eyes shut real tight the ends of his pistols would flash bright like fire and so too would his eyes beneath the brim of his wide black hat. Gingerly, heart racing, I would reach out and lift the brim, wanting to stare upon his hard-looking face again. For there had been a certain kindness, like that of a strict father chastising his wayward daughter. He could be mean, cruel sometimes, but he did it out of love – a perverse kinda protection. In the darkness, as my fingertips dared to push back his hat, it wasn't the man I could see staring back at me, but the wolf. His face bristling with fur and black whiskers, eyes bright and penetrating.

As his lips rolled back into a snarl, I would snap open my eyes, my naked body glistening with feverish sweat as I lay beneath the sheets of my bed. In the dark and to the soundtrack of Sally's bone-rattling orgasms coming from the room next door, I would light yet another cigarette. With the smoke lingering around my shaking fingers, I struggled with those images of the preacher. Although they scared and confused me and made me feel like I was losing my mind, I wanted to hold on to them. Those memories reminded me that what I had experienced back in 1888 was real. If that was real, so were vampires and so was Harry Turner. I didn't want to forget him.

Since returning from 1888 to a life studying criminology and sharing rooms with a nymphomaniac, I'd spent all of my free time hanging out at the place I went back to – was taken back to – in 1888. Now I spent more time at Aldgate Tube Station than I did at my own flat. I even skipped lessons to come here and travel around on the Circle Line, hoping I would see him again – the man who had slipped his arm around my neck and sent me back to 1888. Who was he? What did he look like? I didn't know the answer to either of those questions.

I had followed him on to the Tube train that night because I suspected he was a vampire. I was sure he was responsible for the spate of horrific Jack the Ripper-style killings that had recently taken place in the Whitechapel area. Alone on the late-night train as it rattled through the tunnels beneath the city, I saw a pale-faced man at the window. But he wasn't at the window, it was his reflection. He was standing right behind me the whole time.

Before I had the chance to get away, the man grabbed me from behind, slipping his arm like a vice around my throat. His clothes smelled old and musty – he smelled dead.

"Why are you following me?" he breathed in my ear. His breath felt ice-cold against my cheek.

"I know what you are," I choked.

"And what is that?" he whispered.

"You're a vampire," I gasped, trying to break free of his grip. I wanted to twist around so as to see his face. But he was too strong. With his free hand, he ran a long, white, bony finger down the length of my cheek. His fingernail felt like a blade.

"Oh, Sammy, you don't remember," he almost seemed to chuckle in my ear.

"How do you know my name?"

Just like now, I had with me a cross and a small bottle of holy water. I slowly fished the bottle from the pocket of the coat I was wearing.

"How quickly you have forgotten," he teased me, his breath as stale and old as his coat.

The carriage lights flickered out and, seizing my chance, I jerked my arm backwards, throwing the holy water into his face. I heard him chuckle softly again, and the lights came back on.

"Sammy, you really don't know who I am, do you?" he asked.

I knew he was smiling, and that smile was full of pointed

teeth. "Holy water doesn't work, nor does the garlic I can smell in your pocket, nor the crucifix that glistens between your breasts."

"What have I forgotten?" I wheezed, as his grip became almost suffocating.

"Let me show you," he whispered as the train rattled into Liverpool Street Station and the carriage filled with bright white light.

That's how I went back last time, exactly a year ago today. If I was to be taken back again, then wouldn't it be today? I wondered – or was it that I hoped? The man said I had forgotten and I think now I understood what he meant. Was I forgetting all over again? Perhaps being taken back to 1888 wasn't the only occasion I had gone back in time? Maybe I'd done it before? Wouldn't that explain how I knew how to handle a gun, ride a horse and fight like something close to Jason Bourne on crack? Perhaps I'd just forgotten those other times, so every trip back felt like the first. But this time I refused to forget the preacher and his pack of vampire seekers. This time I would remember them and what happened to me there. However many cigarettes it took to keep me remembering – I would never forget. But I *was* forgetting, however much I tried not to.

As I stood for hours in the rain outside Aldgate Tube Station and scanned the faces of the early-morning commuters and late-night partygoers for my friends, I couldn't be sure I would recognise them again, even if

I did see one of their faces in the crowd. And however much part of me tried to say they weren't real and were just an elaborate fantasy I had created, there was a voice I just couldn't shake from inside my head. It was like I could hear Harry whispering in my ear, *Keep your eyes closed: if you look at me, this isn't real – it's just a fantasy.*

Fantasy or not, Harry had been a real part of what happened to me. And in my heart I knew it was him I sought more than any of the others. I wanted more from my life than marriage and motherhood. I wanted adventure and I'd had that with Harry. He'd excited me – just like those guys excited Sally in her room. And that's why I would rather stand in the cold and rain outside a Tube station than listen to her cries of pleasure. They reminded me too much of what I'd shared with Harry on that steam train as we raced up into the snow-flecked mountains of Colorado seeking out vampires together. And although I wanted to be reminded of everything else, I didn't want to be reminded of what Harry and I had shared, because the thought of not ever experiencing that again made my heart ache.

I pitched out my cigarette and reached inside my coat pocket for another. My fingers touched the rosary beads I had found on the floor of the chapel in the town of Black Water Gap back in 1888. I carried the rosary beads with me everywhere I went. They were a link to my past – they connected me to it like a chain. They were another reminder that what happened was real and not some fantasy. I let the wooden beads and crucifix slide through my cold fingers. I pushed the small bottle of holy water to one side and took out the cigarette packet. I popped a smoke into the corner of my mouth and lit it. Drawing in a hot lungful of smoke, I knocked my bedraggled blond fringe from out of my eyes. I was cold and wet through from the rain. It had been dark now for a few hours as the winter evening drew in. Buses and black cabs hissed past, spraying the pavement with dirty rainwater. Commuters poured off the wet streets and down into the underground station. Some of those passing by cast me a wary eye, suspecting – I guess by my dishevelled look – that I was homeless and begging for money. Others put a hand over their mouths and noses in protest at the smoke I blew into their paths.

My suspicion suddenly proved justified as I heard a clatter at my feet. I glanced down to see several coins splashing into the puddles. Looking up, I caught sight of the man who had tossed them in my direction. His back was to me, the sides of his face hidden behind the collar of his long dark coat, pulled up about his throat. His hair was wet and lank, and hung over his collar.

"Hey!" I called after him. He didn't turn back and disappeared among the melee of passengers heading into the station.

Bending at the knees, I reached down and plucked up several of the coins. At once I could see that they were old. They appeared to be made of aluminium. The writing on them wasn't English. Each of the coins had the phrase *bon pour* written on them. My French wasn't great but I knew the words meant "good for". The coins were very old francs, but why would anyone throw them at me? They looked way too old to be some loose change that a recent traveller from France might be keen to be rid of. Besides, even if they had been new, the franc had gone of circulation years ago.

Flicking my half-smoked cigarette to the kerb, and the ancient coins jiggling in my hand, I went into the station in search of the man who had thrown them at my feet. Passengers jostled with one another as they tried to squeeze through the automated barriers to reach the stairs leading down to the platforms. Knocking my wet fringe from my blue eyes again, I scanned the crowds but couldn't see the man. I pushed my way forward much to the annoyance of other travellers gathered around me.

"Watch where you're treading!" one woman yelped as I crushed her foot beneath my boots.

"There's a queue here!" a portly guy of about fifty with a bulbous red nose barked as I squeezed past him towards the barrier line.

Then, just ahead, I saw the guy who had dropped the coins shuffle through the barrier gates.

"Hey, you!" I called after him. He didn't look back.

Ducking under the arm of a suited man, I inched my way towards the barriers. I pulled my Oyster card from my back jeans pocket and, barging another commuter out of the way, I slapped it against the circular reader. The barrier opened like a set of plastic arms before me and I raced through. Both north and south platforms were crammed full of people. My eyes darted left then right. I saw him, cutting his way through the crowds on the southbound platform. His back was to me and I still couldn't see his face. But it was the man who had thrown me the ancient francs I now gripped in my cold fist.

"Excuse me," I wheezed, pushing through the crowds. "Please, just let me through."

Reaching the top of the stairs, I peered over the shoulders of those gathered before me and looked down. The man was heading towards the platform edge. I caught a fleeting glimpse of his profile before he turned his head away. My heart thumped hard in my chest as it began to quicken. Although I saw his face only briefly, it was pale and drawn, just like the reflection I had seen in the carriage window exactly a year ago. Had he come back? And who was he? This was my chance to find out.

"Let me through," I gasped, pushing forward. Several people in front of me staggered precariously at the top of the stairs.

"Watch it!" A middle-aged woman with too much lipstick on glared back at me.

"Sorry," I whispered, forcing myself past her anyway. I hadn't wasted a whole year of my life hanging out at this station to let the moment pass. I wasn't going to let a woman who looked as if she'd been stung on the arse by a wasp get in my way. After almost clambering over those on the stairs before me, I reached the platform. Stepping sideways, I zigzagged through people waiting for the next Tube train. Pausing for just a moment, I placed my hands on the shoulders of a guy standing directly in front of me and forced myself up on to tiptoe. He glanced over his shoulder at me. I smiled at him and he smiled back. Now why couldn't everyone be like that?

"Hey, sweetheart," he beamed. Before he had a chance to progress his best chat-up line, I was off again, weaving through the crowds towards the edge of the platform where the man with the gaunt and pale face now stood. Using my arms like a set of giant prongs, I worked my way to the very edge of the platform. I looked left then quickly right. He had gone. A train rushed into the station, the gush of wind it created blowing my hair off my shoulders. The Tube's headlamps shone bright white. I raised my arm to shield my eyes and was shoved hard in the back. I teetered on the platform edge. Screaming, and with my arms pinwheeling, I fell into the path of the approaching Tube train . . .

Paris, 9 November 1922

. . . with my arms pinwheeling, I staggered backwards, nearly spilling the champagne from the glass I held in my hand. I could hear laughter and the sound of jazz music. Smoke filled the air, but it wasn't smog – it was cigarette smoke. The air was pungent with it.

"Steady on," I heard someone laugh. A hand gently took my arm. "I think you've perhaps had too much to drink."

The voice was male. Although I understood perfectly what he said, the man spoke in French.

"I'm fine," I said, raising my free hand to my brow and pressing fingertips to my temple. It was then I realised that I too was speaking in French. I was thinking in English but talking in French. When had I ever learned to speak French? I had never been to France and what little of the language I had mastered at school was basic and most of that I had forgotten.

"*Vous avez besoin d'air frais,*" I heard the man say. And I understood him perfectly. "You need some fresh air," he had said.

Yes, perhaps, I thought, and the words came out of my mouth, "*Oui, peut-être.*"

How had this happened and where was I? Teetering backwards again, and feeling dizzy, I looked about the room. Just like the underground platform had been crowded, so too was the bar I now found myself in. A small jazz band was playing in the corner and all around the edge of the room were tables with candles, men and women gathered about them. They were all speaking in French and the whole room felt charged with a sense of excitement and anticipation. At the centre of the club was a dance floor and gathered on it were men and women doing the Charleston, kicking out their heels in time to the music and twisting their hips. I couldn't help but notice how young and strangely boyish the women looked. They had short hair crimped into neat finger waves to the sides of their heads or cut into neat bobs. Others wore close-fitting hats and sleeveless dresses that made them appear flat-chested with slim narrow hips. Most of the dresses were strapless. They were short enough to flap just above the knee as the women danced, offering a flash of leg and silk stockings. I knew at once that these women were flappers and I was at a petting party. How did I know that? I couldn't be sure and my brain felt too muddled to figure it out. How had I known how to ride a horse and handle a gun back in 1888? I just did, just like I now knew that "flapper" was a name given to a certain kind of young woman in the 1920s. These women liked to wear short skirts and listen and dance to jazz. They were considered impetuous by those older in society who disliked their excessive taste for make-up, alcohol, casual sex, smoking and driving cars. They appeared to flout the social and sexual norms of the time. I couldn't help but think that Sally would have made a great flapper. She would have loved to be a young woman during the Roaring Twenties in Paris. But was I in Paris and had I travelled back in time to the 1920s? And if so, why? Wasn't this just another of my fantasies?

"Come on, let's take in some air," the man whispered in my ear over the sound of the music. He took the glass of champagne from my hand and I looked into his face for the first time. He was clean-shaven with a firm jawline. He had dark eyes and black hair swept back from his brow. He could only have been a few years older than me, which would make him about twenty-five. As far as I was concerned, I had never seen him before and had no idea who he was or what his name was. The young man who now guided me around the edge of the smoky dance floor wore a dark-blue single-breasted suit jacket. His trousers were pleated at the waist and cuffed at the bottom.

He wore a black bowtie. He walked with a swagger as he guided me towards the door of the club.

With my head still spinning, I tried to figure out where I was. I eased my arm from his grip and looked at him.

"Do I know you?" I frowned, the words coming out in fluent French once again. "What is your name?"

He looked at me with a boyish smile. "Sammy, we've been dancing all night long. Of course you know me. I think you've had more champagne than I first thought."

"But . . ." I started, not knowing what to say or even what to ask next. Before I could gather my thoughts, I saw a face in the crowd that I did recognise. My heart stopped in my chest. Harry Turner was standing on the other side of the bar talking to a beautiful young woman. In fact he was more than just talking to her. He was leaning in close, so their noses almost touched, lips just a whisper apart. My heart thudded into action again and I felt sick. The woman was dressed like the others crowded into the bar. From her slender fingers dangled a cigarette in a long thin black holder. I reached into my pocket, in sudden need of a smoke myself. But my pocket wasn't there and neither was my coat. I looked down and for the first time realised I was no longer wearing my denim jeans and long dark coat but a pretty cream dress that hung just above my stocking-covered knees. The dress was sleeveless and hung from my shoulders by two thin straps. My shoulders! They felt different. It took a moment to realise what it was that made them feel so different: my hair wasn't cascading over them. Slowly, I raised my hands and felt the small bucket-type hat that now covered my short bobbed hair. It had been cut.

"My hair," I whispered, looking back at the man. "What has happened to my hair?"

He frowned curiously at me. "Your hair looks beautiful." Then, reaching out with his hand, he gently ran his fingertips down the curve of my neck. His touch was cold and my skin became peppered with gooseflesh. "Your skin is like silk," he said, leaning in close and brushing his lips against the side of my neck.

Although my first instinct was to flinch away, I felt rooted to the spot as I stared over his shoulder at Harry. He was running a hand down the curve of the young woman's back and over the swell of her tight little arse. My mind immediately threw up a memory of Harry pulling me naked from a river back in 1888. He had held me in very much the same way he was holding the woman on the other side of the bar. His fingers had lingered over my arse back then too. A pang of jealousy stung me hard at the sight of him pawing another woman. But hang on! What was I doing getting jealous over a guy I had probably created in my own imagination? I mean, how did shit like that happen? I was most likely creating this very fantasy as I lay dying beneath the wheels of the Tube train back in London in 2013. If this whole bar, the dancing flappers and Harry were indeed my own fantasy, I wasn't going to get jealous. That wasn't how this was meant to work – was it? Shouldn't I be in control of my fantasy? That's why it was a fantasy. I wasn't jealous of the woman in Harry's arms. I was jealous of Sally and all the fun she seemed to have. Hadn't I always been jealous of her? That's why I had invented the journey back to 1888 where I had mind-blowing sex with a cowboy. And here I was again, dying beneath a Tube train, the last currents of electricity going through my tangled web of a brain, creating one last fantasy. I was in the swinging twenties, with a hot-looking guy on my arm, drinking champagne in the most romantic city in the world. And if that fantasy wasn't hot enough, my dying brain had thrown in the cowboy to really get my heart racing before it stopped altogether. But that's what was wrong. Harry wasn't dressed as a cowboy. Sure, he still had the unkempt sandy hair and the lower half of his rugged face was still covered with stubble, but the jeans, chaps and woven shirt were all gone. Now he stood in a sporty-looking suit and a white shirt and tie.

I pulled away from the guy who was still petting my neck and rubbed my temples again with my fingertips. I had a sudden thought of the moody and arrogant Harry stepping on to the dance floor and doing the Charleston. Now why wasn't that in this fantasy I had created? Because that would've been funny – not sexy. From over the shoulder of the guy before me, I watched Harry lean back from the young woman he had been groping. Taking her by the arm, he led her towards the door and out into the night.

"I think I need some fresh air after all," I said to my unknown companion and headed towards the door, a small sequined clutch bag swinging from my arm.

A light drizzle sparkled in the glow of a nearby gas lamp. The street I stood in was cobbled. The night air was crisp and I wrapped my arms about my bare shoulders and shivered. This part of the city appeared eerily quiet, the only sound the music and laughter coming from the club. It was like the flappers were the only people alive. In the distance I heard the echo of a church bell chime three times. I felt the stranger's arm snake about me as he pulled me close. Who was this guy and what did he want? But it wasn't him I was really interested in – it was Harry. I looked left down the cobbled street and saw him walking away, hand in hand with the woman. He said something to her and I heard her laughter float back towards me. Harry had never held my hand and had definitely never made me laugh. He had always been too moody and sullen for that.

"I'd like to take a walk," I said, slipping free from the guy's hold on me. The sound of the laughter and jazz music faded away as we left the club behind.

The man walked beside me in the rain. He pulled his collar up and I glanced at him as I followed Harry and the woman. "Where exactly are we?"

"The Left Bank," he said, with another frown as if I should know.

"Left Bank?" I cocked a finely pencilled eyebrow at him.

"The home of Hemingway, Matisse and Picasso. We're in Paris, Samantha Carter." He turned on the spot and pointed into the distance. "Beautiful, no?"

Teetering on my heels, I turned round and gasped. Over the tops of the buildings that lined the narrow street, I could see the illuminated point of the Eiffel Tower. "Yes, beautiful," I breathed.

"And romantic?" the man said, sliding his arm around my shoulder again.

I slipped away with a shrug and a smile, turning to see Harry disappear into an alleyway further down the street. Fearing I might lose sight of him again after all this time and wanting to catch up with him once more before the paramedics back in London peeled my burned flesh from the electric rail beneath the Tube train and bagged and tagged me, I started after him again. The stranger followed. I felt nervous and sick in the pit of my stomach. Would Harry remember me? Had he forgotten me like I'd nearly forgotten him? Did he remember what we shared back in 1888? Or had I been replaced already? I opened the small clutch bag and found a cigarette case and lighter. There was a cigarette holder too, but I left that in the bottom of the bag. I lit a cigarette, blowing a thick cloud of smoke into the damp night air. Then, as I placed the case and lighter back into the clutch bag, my fingers brushed against something that felt vaguely familiar. I peered inside and could see the rosary beads and a small glass bottle of holy water. Lying next to them were the coins that had been dropped at my feet outside Aldgate Tube Station. I glanced sideways at the man walking beside me. The rain had given his once-neat swept-back hair a bedraggled look, just like the man I had followed on to the platform. Was he the man who threw me those francs? Who shoved me in the back and in front of the approaching train? Had he come back too? He glanced sideways at me and smiled. I looked away.

We reached the entrance of the alleyway and I peered round the edge of the wall. The alleyway walls were black and slick with rain. I screwed my eyes half shut and gazed into the darkness and my heart leaped. The beautiful young flapper had Harry pressed against the wall and was smothering his face and neck in kisses. I felt that pang of jealousy again and it was like a blow to the stomach. I tried to shake the feeling away. I refused to be jealous of a woman I had created in my own fantasy. And as the feeling ebbed away, it was replaced with another. A sense of unease. Something wasn't quite right. It wasn't just that I was in the middle of Paris on a rain-drenched night sometime in the 1920s –there was something else too. My survival instincts suddenly became sharper – more focused. I found myself looking into the alleyway, up at the slick walls and then over my shoulder. My brain was trying to figure out the safest and quickest way of escape should I need it. Looking for anything in the rain-swollen gutters that I could use as a weapon. I glanced back into the eyes of the man now blocking the entrance of the alleyway and my only way out. A smile stretched across his pale face and my heart rate quickened.

I looked back at Harry as the flapper continued to kiss and suck at his neck . . .

All of my instincts suddenly burned brightly at once and the world seemed to slow down.

"Harry!" I screamed as the flapper threw back her head, her red gums now full of sharpened points. The young woman no longer looked beautiful, but hideous. Her face was almost torn in two, where her mouth stretched open revealing a mass of fangs. She lunged at Harry's neck. But it was as if he had been expecting it, because he darted to the right, one of his strong hands stretching into a claw. He buried this deep into the flapper's throat, slicing her neck open almost to the point of decapitation. As thick jets of black blood spurted from her throat, Harry snapped his head to the left and looked straight at me. His once-blue eyes burned like two suns.

"Behind you," he snarled.

Spinning round, and not knowing why, I reached beneath the hem of my dress, ran my fingers over the lacy top of my left stocking and pulled out the small silver dagger that was concealed there. I did this with such speed that in an eye blink the dagger was in my fist and I was burying it in the chest of the man who had led me from the bar. I don't know who looked more surprised, me or him, at the sight of the blood gushing from the gaping wound I had made in him. How had the dagger got beneath my dress? But how had a pair of gleaming pistols ended up around my waist in 1888? I didn't know the answer to either question. With the man's mouth beginning to stretch open across his white face like a crimson gash, I had a flash-shot memory of the vampire bandits I fought and killed back in 1888. Their mouths had gaped as if the lower halves of their faces had been sliced open with a razor blade and stuffed full of broken and jagged fangs.

The vampire who now stood before me screeched and grabbed for the hilt of the dagger that was buried in his chest. With it still gripped in my fist, I twisted it hard to the right, skewering his heart. A jet of acid like bile sprayed from the vampire's throat, as it threw back its head in agony. I pulled the dagger free, black clots of blood dripping from its serrated edge. The vampire crumpled before me, its knees sinking into the puddles that covered the cobbled street. As his cries of pain faded and death took him, the night became alive with ear-piercing shrieks of rage. I looked along the street to see the doorway of the club swing violently open. Several of the flappers sprang out into the rain. I could hear the faint sound of jazz music over their cries. The once-beautiful young girls looked in my direction. Then, tilting back their heads on their slender white necks, they sniffed the air. I glanced down at the blood still dripping from the dagger in my fist. Slowly, they straightened their heads and looked at me, their eyes glowing bright. The red metallic-like lipstick daubed on their perfect lips seemed to stretched across their faces as if being smeared by invisible fingers. With fangs glistening from ear to ear, the flappers raced over the cobbled street towards me.

"Run!" Harry roared from beside me.

I looked at him; his eyes still shone fiercely and thick sideburns covered his face where moments ago there had just been heavy stubble. His hair was thicker and messier too somehow and both of his fists were giant claws, each of his fingers capped with long ivory-looking nails.

"Run where?" I hollered over the sound of the screeching vampires coming towards us.

"I have a car," he said, tearing away.

"A car?" I called after him. "No horse this time round?"

"So you do remember something," he shot back over his shoulder. It was then for the first time I realised that his American accent had gone and he was speaking perfect French like me. Now *that* was hot. Thank God the part of my mind that conjured up these fantasies had got something right. A French-speaking and -sounding Harry – you've got to be kidding me. I suddenly couldn't help but wonder what he would sound like in the throes of passion. You know, like when he reached the point of no return and yelled out . . .

"Are you gonna stand there thinking about cock all

night long or what?" Harry roared as if able to read my mind.

"I wasn't thinking about cock," I lied, starting after him down the street.

"Really?" he seemed to sneer sideways at me. "As far as I can remember you were always thinking about cock."

"No, I wasn't," I shot back. "It was you who had sex on the brain. And as far as I can remember you couldn't keep you filthy hands off me—"

"That's not how I remember it, doll," he cut in, the vampire flappers just yards away now.

"And stop calling me that!" I snapped at him. We had only been back in each other's company mere moments and we were already arguing. I hadn't forgotten that.

Harry stopped before a long gleaming silver car parked at the kerb. It didn't have a roof, but had black leather seats back and front. A large spare wheel was fixed to the side.

Harry bounded in and sat behind the steering wheel. "Get in," he barked.

"But it's got no roof," I said, clambering in beside him.

"This is a Rolls-Royce Silver Ghost," he snapped with some pride.

"Is that meant to mean something to me?" I said, glancing right to see several of the flappers springing into the air at us. "I think I preferred the horse."

With a deafening screech, Harry sped the car away from the kerb and the flappers. This part of the city seemed abandoned, like everyone had fled. Apart from us, there were no people on the streets and no cars. It was like everyone else had shut themselves behind locked doors for the night. And with the vampires behind us, I couldn't blame them for doing so. I glanced back and saw that they were coming on freakishly fast, their movements awkward and jerky-looking.

"Can't this thing go any faster?" I yelled, staring over my shoulder at the vampires racing down the centre of the narrow road behind us.

"Fifty is all it's got," Harry shouted, pressing the pedal flat to the floor.

"Perhaps I should get out and push?" I shot back.

Ignoring me, and keeping his eyes on the gas-lit roads ahead, Harry took one hand from the wheel and plunged it between my legs.

"What do you think you're doing?" I squealed, clamping my thighs tight against his wandering hand. "I don't think now is the time for your fun and games!"

"The dagger," he breathed. "You're meant to have a dagger concealed in the top of your stockings. That was the plan."

"The plan?" I looked at him, eyes wide. "What plan?"

"To break up this nest of vampires," he said, wiggling his fingers about beneath the hem of my dress. I crushed his hand between my thighs as it pawed at my stocking tops. "The flappers?" he said, glancing at me. "The vampires have started to breed in Paris. Most came here after being infected in the Great War . . ." He stopped and gazed at my blank expression.

I gazed back at him.

Then, pulling his fingers free from between my legs, he gripped the wheel with both hands again. "Sammy, you can't keep forgetting like this." He sounded pissed off at me again.

"Forgetting what?" I breathed, the vampires screeching right behind us now. What had I forgotten?

"Once was bad enough," Harry groaned. "The preacher told us to be patient with you. But we've had this fucking operation planned for months. We've followed these arseholes across Russia, Italy and into France. We were to go into the club tonight. We were both meant to pick someone up, lure them out of the club and see if they were vam—"

The back of the car suddenly shook, causing it to lurch across the road. Both of us looked behind to see two of the vampire flappers were climbing over the back of the car. Their eyes were black like stones, their lips red and gums bleeding a white gooey pus. Their dresses flapped about their knees and I couldn't help but see the irony.

"Perhaps now would be a good time to use the dagger," Harry shouted, glancing at it gleaming in my fist.

I looked down at the blade, then back at Harry. "You knew it was in my hand the whole time," I breathed.

"No, I never," he said, swinging the car left then right as if to shake free the vampires that were scampering all over the back of the car.

"Yes, you did," I gasped. "You just wanted to stick your hand up my dress!"

"And why would I want to do a thing like that?" Harry barked.

"Because you're a fucking pervert, that's why!" I yelled back at him. "And like I said, you can't keep your filthy paws off me!"

"Don't flatter yourself, sweetheart," he shot back. "Now are you gonna sit there fantasising about me or deal with the vampires who are about to rip our heads clean off?"

"Argh!" I roared in frustration. "Why do you have to be so freaking difficult the whole time?" Spinning around in my seat, I shot my right hand forward and buried the dagger into the eye socket of the nearest flapper. Her eye squirted out around the hilt of the dagger like a pool of black tar. I pulled the blade free as the flapper toppled lifelessly from the car and into the road to bounce into the gutter. Another of the flappers pounced over the backseat of the car, a purple tongue lolling from the corner of her mouth as she licked her bloated lips. Her claws rose like a set of knives and she lunged at me. I swiped the dagger through the air, slicing her claws free at the knuckles. They fell away into the footwell. Harry was swerving left and right across the road. As I watched the vampire suck up the blood pumping from its bleeding stumps, another loomed over the spare wheel on the side of the car. She grabbed my wrist and I cried out in pain. It felt like every bone in my arm was about to disintegrate into powder. The dagger flew from my grasp and clattered away beneath the wheels of the car. With the vehicle lurching left and right, I tried to shake the vampire free, but her hold was vice-like. Rocking back my head, I shot forward again, smashing my forehead into the bridge of the flapper's nose. There was a crunching sound as her nose broke. She screeched in pain, her black eyes rolling up into their sockets. Letting go of my wrist, she dropped back over the side of the car. I peered over the spare wheel and saw she had sunk her claws into the runner. Her legs trailed out behind her as she was dragged along the cobbled road. She was wailing and screeching in pain, but refused to let go. Lapping up the black blood gushing from her nose and into her cavernous mouth, she looked up at me and started to pull herself up the door. I pulled at the handle and kicked the door open. The wind caught it and dragged me from my seat. I was thrown clear and just like the vampire moments before, I hung from the side of the car as my legs trailed along the street.

"Harry!" I screamed, as another of the vampires saw my desperate plight and came racing alongside the car.

Harry glanced down at me. He flung out his hand. I gripped it at the wrist, my knuckles glowing white. He heaved me back into my seat.

"I've lost my dagger," I told him, as he swung the car on to a wider road that ran parallel to the River Seine.

"I have one in my pocket," he said, looking at me.

"Give it to me, then," I said, holding out a hand and glancing back in fear over my shoulder. The last of the flappers, the one without fingers, had managed to get to her feet and was running alongside the car inches from me. Her face was a contorted mask of hatred and anger. Bile sprayed from her fangs and back into the night. Behind her the Eiffel Tower stood silhouetted against a half moon that peeked from behind a bank of cloud.

"It's in my pocket," Harry bellowed as he raced the car along the bank of the Seine. The water looked black and choppy. "Take it! I'm trying to drive here!" He raised his butt off the car seat to make it easier for me to slide my hand into his trouser pocket. I pushed my hand inside and beneath the fabric of his trousers, I could feel his hard thigh muscles. There was no dagger, so I pushed deeper into his pocket until my fingertips touched something else which was just as hard as his thigh muscle. I quickly pulled my hand free.

"There's no dagger in there," I said, looking at him. "That pocket is empty."

"Of course it's empty." He glanced at me. "The dagger is in my jacket pocket."

"But you said it was in your trouser pocket," I scowled.

"No, I never," he said, looking forward again. "Like I said, you just can't stop thinking about my—"

"Not yours," I cut in, reaching inside his jacket and finding the dagger there. Curling my fingers around its cold metal hilt, I pulled it out. Spinning around in my seat and taking aim in an instant, I pulled back my arm and drove the dagger forward, burying it in the vampire's forehead, slicing into her brain with such force that she flew back as if snatched away. With her dying screams ringing in my ears, I dropped back into my seat and faced the front again.

"You know you're such a jerk," I said, still feeling mad at Harry.

"Thanks," he muttered, steering the car off the main drag and into the narrower back roads.

And although he drove me half-crazy, I couldn't help but feel exhilarated now I was back with him. I craved the adventure we were sharing once again. But where were the others? Where was the preacher, Louise and Zoe? Before I had the chance to ask Harry their whereabouts, he was bringing the car to a stop outside a small hotel. Bounding from his seat, he looked back at me and said, "C'mon."

With the clutch bag hanging once again from my shoulder, I followed Harry into the hotel. Perhaps the others would be meeting us here? I wondered, crossing the small lobby. The floor gleamed with polish and a crystal chandelier hung high above.

A bald-headed and bespectacled man sat behind a wooden counter, a key cabinet fixed to the wall behind him. Harry nodded in the porter's direction.

"*Bonjour*," the man said in recognition.

"*Bonjour*," I smiled back. Lowering my head, I followed

Harry quickly up the stairs on the other side of the lobby.

When we reached a carpeted landing, Harry fished a key from his suit jacket pocket. He stopped before a door and looked left then right as if to make sure we hadn't been followed. Once he was certain we were alone, he slipped the key into the lock and pushed open the door. I followed him into the room and he closed the door behind us.

I watched Harry cross to the window, where he drew the curtains shut. The room had a small sofa and a chair, a basin in the corner and a large four-poster bed. It didn't appear that Harry and the team were short of money in the 1920s. With my back to the door, I stood and watched Harry pull off his jacket and tie. He threw both into the armchair. The hair about his face had gone now, as had his claws.

"You might as well make yourself comfortable," he said in that delicious French accent again. "The preacher and the others haven't arrived yet."

"How can you be so sure?" I asked, suddenly feeling too timid to step fully into the room.

"Because I can't hear the preacher and Louise fucking in the room next door," he said, pouring whisky into two glasses.

"I'd forgotten about that," I said, as he crossed the room towards me.

He shoved one of the glasses into my hand. He drank, his eyes never leaving mine as he peered at me over the rim of his glass.

"That's not all you seem to have forgotten," he said.

I sipped the whisky and grimaced. I would never get used to the taste of it. "I remember drinking whisky with you on that train. The Scorpion Steam, I think it was called."

"I'm not talking about remembering drinking whisky with me," he said.

"What are you talking about then?" I asked, my heart starting to beat a little faster. His towering presence and the way his eyes never left mine was a little intimidating.

"You don't want to remember," he said, then took another gulp of his drink. He wiped it from his lips.

"I tried to remember," I said. "I wanted to remember you, the preacher and what happened to us back in 1888 . . ."

"That's not what I'm talking about," he grunted. "You don't remember who you really are. The preacher says you're still too scared to remember."

"What are you talking about?" I asked, shaking my head. "You're confusing me, Harry."

"Try to concentrate for once, Sammy, and you'll remember," he said, narrowing the gap between us so I could feel his whisky breath against my face.

"Remember what?" I whispered as he leaned into me, his cheek brushing against mine.

Then, for the second time that night, I felt his hand slide up beneath the hem of my dress. But this time I didn't clamp my thighs shut on his hand. I felt the ball of his thumb glide over me. "You're too damn wet to concentrate," he whispered in my ear. "You have something else on your mind."

"What?" I breathed in his ear, fighting the urge to shudder at his touch.

"This," he said, taking his hand from between my legs and tearing at my dress. He ripped the straps free, the dress sliding down over my hips and forming a puddle of silk around my feet. Harry looked at my breasts, then down over my stomach and at the tiny tangle of blond hair between my legs. I could see hunger in his eyes and it turned me on. Knowing he wanted me as much as I wanted him made me wetter still. It was like he hadn't eaten in years and had come across a banquet – a banquet of flesh.

Making a fist, he lost his fingers in my short hair and yanked me towards him. He crushed his lips over mine, pushing his tongue into my mouth. I welcomed it, pushing and entwining my own tongue with his. I pulled open his shirt and felt his hair brush against my hard nipples. The coarseness of it just made them harder. I felt a heightened sense of excitement. Tonight this wasn't just me lying in the dark of my small room, back in 2013, stroking myself as I fought to remember what Harry and I had once shared. Tonight I wouldn't come alone, with the sound of Sally and her latest fuck echoing in my ears from the room next door. Tonight Harry and I would come together, the only cries of pleasure I would hear would be our own. With his shirt now open, I struggled to get it free. I was desperate to feel his naked chest against mine. I wanted to feel the whole of him pressed against me. He shrugged his broad shoulders and his shirt fell away. Breaking our kiss, I smothered his chest in kisses. Slinking down before him, I undid his trouser belt. And, wanting to be free as much I wanted him to be, Harry took hold of my hands in his and helped me unfasten his trousers. He pressed the flats of my hands against him as if to show me how hard I had made him. Curling my fingers around the length of his cock, I brushed my lips over the end of it. Harry buried his hands in my hair. I glanced up into his hungry eyes again. Now I was hungry and I took him – all of him. With his hands lost in my hair, he guided my head slowly back and forth, but I needed no encouragement.

As he guided me faster and faster over him, he looked down into my face and said, "I want you, but not like this."

Taking my lips from over him, I looked into his face and whispered, "How then?"

Without saying anything more, Harry pushed me down on to the sofa, not the bed like I had been expecting. He ran his strong hands over my thighs and ankles, pushing my legs apart. As he came forward, I sank my fingertips into his firm arse.

"Take me," I begged, just wanting to feel again like he had made me feel on that train.

"I'm going to take you all right," he snarled.

"Oh yeah," I shuddered, feeling the tip of him brush over me before he sank between my legs.

Gripping my stocking-covered thighs with his fingers, he dragged me partway off the sofa, so he could push himself deeper into me. I cried out as a knot of pleasure began to tighten inside me. I squeezed gently closed around him and I felt him grow harder at the sensation of my tightening muscles.

"That feels so good," he groaned, and I liked the sudden sense of power I felt I had over him. "You make me feel so fucking horny."

"How horny?" I teased, opening my legs wider for him. "Show me."

As if sensing how much I wanted him, Harry gripped hold of my arse in one hand and placed the other in the small of my back. I arched off the sofa, grinding my hips forwards and up, keen to take as much of him as possible. The sofa rocked violently beneath us as we fucked. We rocked frantically against each other as our pace quickened.

I cried out, my whole body shuddering as I got closer and closer, each of his strokes making me wetter and hotter, my breathing rapid gasps. It felt as if an unbearable force were building inside of me, waiting to spill over.

"Harder," I gasped, the throbbing between my legs growing stronger, my body glimmering with a fine sheen of sweat. I didn't know for how much longer I could stave off the inevitable moment when that explosion of deep ecstasy would rush through my body. But the need to let go was becoming unbearable and the desire to feel that upsurge of pleasure was making me something close to delirious.

Harry pushed himself harder and deeper into me. As if he could sense how close I was. But my heightened excitement only seemed to add to his own as he rocked between my legs.

With that wave of indescribable lust beginning to unravel deep within me, I cried out. The feeling was like an unbearable desire I wanted to last for an eternity. Writhing beneath him, I let out a frantic series of moans. "Harry, I'm coming," I gasped.

I threw my head backwards, sinking my fingernails into the arms of the sofa. My whole body shuddered, the sensations rushing through me too much to bear. With my eyes scarcely open, I looked up into Harry's face and, just like on the train, he was like some kind of wild beast. His face was a mask of anger or agonising ecstasy, I couldn't be sure. He jerked suddenly, his powerful hips rocking back and forth. He threw his head back and something close to a desperate roar escaped his lips.

I entwined my legs about his back, locking him deep inside of me. The throbbing between my legs was slowly weakening but I didn't want him to leave me until it had gone completely. Harry dropped forward and I held him in my arms and felt suddenly fearful that he might just leave me like he had before.

"I never want this to end," I whispered, covering his face in gentle kisses. "I never want to forget it."

"But you will," he whispered, staring into my eyes.

"Help me to remember," I said, and already I felt like I was sinking, drowning in his arms. "I don't want to forget what happened tonight. I don't want to forget you."

Easing me down on to the floor, Harry looked at me. Then without saying anything, he snatched up the small clutch bag I had been carrying. Holding it upside down, he shook the contents all over the floor.

"What are you looking for?" I asked, picking up my dress and covering my breasts with it.

From among the cigarette case, francs and jar of face powder, Harry plucked the rosary beads, the bottle of holy water and the cigarette lighter. With the rosary swinging from his fist, he lit a flame with the lighter and held it to the silver crucifix hanging from the chain. The metal cross started to glow orange, then red, as he heated it.

"What are you doing?" I breathed.

"Turn round," he said.

I did as he said. I felt his fingertips brush over the nape of my neck. "This will help numb the pain," he said.

"What pain?" I frowned, glancing quickly back at him. He was unscrewing the cap from the bottle of holy water.

"Look away," he whispered, his breath warm against my neck as he leaned over me.

I felt a splash of cold as Harry poured some of the holy

water over the back of my neck. It ran like melting ice between my shoulder blades and down my back.

"Is this some kinda weird baptism?" I asked, starting to feel a little freaked out.

"No," he whispered. "I'm just saving your life, Samantha Carter."

There was a blinding white flash of pain as he pressed the seething hot crucifix against the nape of my neck. I cried out in pain and fear as . . .

London, 9 November 2013

. . . the hand gripped the back of my neck and pulled me away from the platform edge.

"Are you trying to kill yourself or something?" a voice said in my ear.

I staggered back on the heels of my boots as the Tube train thundered past just inches from me. Flapping my arms, I fell on my arse with a thud. The train came to a halt at the platform and the doors opened to reveal a vacant carriage. Feeling as if I were coming out of the worst hangover imaginable, I scrambled to my feet and peered along the desolate platform. The sign on the wall read ALDGATE. How did I end up down here? I wondered, rubbing my temples with my fingertips. Just like the platform, each of the train carriages was empty. But that wasn't right. Someone had spoken to me. Someone had pulled me back on to the platform and out of the path of the approaching train. I whirled around, my long black coat flapping about my knees. There was someone – a man – and he was halfway up the stairs leading from the platform out of the station. He wore a long black coat, with the collar pulled up at the neck, as if to hide his face.

"Hey you!" I called after him. He didn't stop climbing the stairs. "What just happened here?"

The man reached the top and stopped. Without looking back, he said, "Mind the gap next time." Then he was moving again, heading out of the station.

I went to go after him, but it was then I heard a clinking sound coming from my coat pocket. I stopped at the foot of the stairs. Slowly, I reached inside. My fingertips brushed over what felt like a collection of coins. I closed my fist around them and pulled them out of my pocket. I uncurled my fist and stared at the francs lying in the palm of my hand.

"Where did they come from?" I frowned.

And however much I tried, I just couldn't remember.

Sammy's adventures continue in 2015!

In the meantime, go back to the beginning . . . back to the West . . .

VAMPIRE SEEKER

Samantha Carter believes a vampire is responsible for the brutal deaths of four women in London and finally she has the chance to catch him. Desperate to prove the killer's identity, she chases him onto a late night tube train. But Samantha doesn't reach the next station – instead she's pulled into a very different journey, back in time to the Wild West – where friendship, desire and even love all come hand in hand with deadly danger.

To stay alive she'll have to work out who to trust – and when to resist temptation. For Sammy's nightmares are about to come true – vampires are real and more lethal than she ever imagined . . .

piatkus